ON WOMEN

On Women

by
CLARA M. THOMPSON

Selected from
INTERPERSONAL PSYCHOANALYSIS

Edited by MAURICE R. GREEN

Foreword by ERICH FROMM

A MERIDIAN BOOK

NEW AMERICAN LIBRARY

NEW YORK AND SCARBOROUGH, ONTARIO

Library of Congress Catalog Card Number: 86-18162

Published by arrangement with Basic Books Inc., Publishers

Previously published in a Mentor edition

 MERIDIAN TRADEMARK REG.U.S. PAT.OFF. AND FOREIGN COUNTRIES
REGISTERED TRADEMARK—MARCA REGISTRADA
HECHO EN BRATTLEBORO, VT., U.S.A.

SIGNET, SIGNET CLASSIC, MENTOR, ONYX, PLUME, MERIDIAN and
NAL BOOKS are published *in the United States* by New American Library,
1633 Broadway, New York, New York 10019, *in Canada by* The New American Library
of Canada Limited, 81 Mack Avenue, Scarborough, Ontario M1L 1M8

First Meridian Printing, September, 1986

1 2 3 4 5 6 7 8 9

PRINTED IN THE UNITED STATES OF AMERICA

CONTENTS

On Women

Preface

The Women's Liberation movement of recent years has given courage and a new sense of self, a fresh perspective and a new identity, to women frightened and confused by the cultural and personal conflicts arising from the rapidly changing conditions and value systems of contemporary Western industrial society. At the same time, however, the movement has tended to oversimplify, seeking the solution to problems of great complexity in a narrow and angry aggressiveness, conceived and expressed in the competitive, dog-eat-dog terms of the commercial marketplace.

Clara Thompson's work is a refreshing antidote to this negative aspect of the Women's Liberation movement, while yet illuminating and defining what is valuable in the movement. In the light of recent findings in the physiology and psychology of women, her contribution stands today as fresh and solid as when it was first written.

No innovator, but rather an astute clinician and inspired practitioner, Clara Thompson nevertheless through her clear grasp of the relevant and useful in the works of others gave great impetus to a major development in psychoanalysis in America—the evolution of recent years from the libido theory of Freud to a humanist, interpersonal psychology, with its more flexible techniques and psychosocial approach.

Her book, *Psychoanalysis: Its Evolution and Development,* was the first effort made by a psychoanalyst to integrate the various theories of Freud, Adler, Jung, Ferenczi, Reich, Sullivan, Fromm, Horney, et al. In her practice, she did not confine herself, as did many of her contemporaries, to merely "suitable" neurotic patients, but recognized the positive potential of many, considered hopeless by her colleagues, whose problems involved conflict with the restraints of conventional society—the homosexual, the single woman, the schizophrenic.

Her central philosophy was a passionate belief in psychoanalysis as an instrument for discovering and developing the true humanity, however submerged or atrophied, of the individual patient. Her emphasis, in practice as in theory, was placed on the sensitive and acute analysis of the interplay between persons in the growth of a human relationship: in short, *interpersonal* psychoanalysis.

One of the first analysts to adopt this approach, Sándor Ferenczi, had been recommended to Clara Thompson by Harry Stack Sullivan, the leading American theoretician in the field of interpersonal relations as a clinical approach. Erich Fromm, leading exponent of the interpersonal approach in social psychology, was her friend, colleague, and analyst. Her critical appraisals of the contributions of Ferenczi, Sullivan, and Fromm, stemming from her close personal involvement with them, are invaluable guides to their work and its significance in psychoanalysis in America.

In her life as in her work, Dr. Thompson represented a freedom of spirit and forcefulness of character that exemplified her own womanhood. Combative in the face of opposition, a feminist in the better sense of the word, she never permitted herself the shrillness or acrimony of the polemicist. Childless, she appreciated fully—perhaps a shade regretfully—the fulfillment that motherhood can bring. Affirming the right of all women to equal opportunity and responsibility with men,

she never made the feminist cause a banner of her own
glorification. She was careful at all times to distinguish
the issues that transcend mere sexual difference in the
struggles that both men and women must make to
fulfill themselves in a disorderly and difficult world.

In this respect, she shunned stereotyped formulations. Unconventional patterns, even homosexuality,
might be the practical optimum for certain women. The
fact was to be accepted: it was not to be projected as a
solution.

The spirit of pragmatic humanism pervaded Clara
Thompson's approach to both men and women. It
softened her Yankee combativeness with a tender concern for relieving the pain and constriction in the lives
of her fellow human beings.

A popular teacher, lecturer, and supervisory analyst,
Dr. Thompson evoked extremes of cultlike loyalty and
bitter opposition in her work. It was characteristic of
her to refuse to be deified, to reject all dogma, and to
share responsibility.

She began her career as a classic psychoanalyst,
teaching other analysts at the conservative New York
Psychoanalytic Institute. In her professional growth,
she often stood against the prevailing authorities and
built on their work. She began with Freud's fundamental contributions despite their unpopularity with her
director, Adolf Meyer, dean of American psychiatry,
while still training at Johns Hopkins. At a later date,
she championed her friend Ferenczi when he lost favor
with Freud and Jones. In the same spirit, she opposed
the Institute in supporting Karen Horney.

Under the appearance of almost naïve simplicity
and femininity, she was a skilled organizer, ingenious
tactician, and eloquent speaker. She frankly enjoyed
prestige and power, and gained a prominent position in
all of the groups in which she participated. She was the
first president of the Washington-Baltimore Psychoanalytic Institute, first vice-president of the American
Association for the Advancement of Psychoanalysis,
first executive director of the William Alanson White

Institute, and a trustee of the Academy of Psychoanalysis.

During the last thirty years of her life, Clara Thompson published fifty-seven papers, articles, interviews, and book reviews, covering a great variety of subject matter, from general concepts in a developing, dynamic interpersonal psychoanalysis to detailed clinical application and critique. In addition to the published works, there were eight unpublished papers and the uncompleted manuscript of a book on the psychology of women.

In editing this considerable body of material for a previous collection, *Interpersonal Psychoanalysis: The Selected Papers of Clara M. Thompson* (Basic Books, Inc., New York, London, 1964), I selected with particular reference to a professional readership, omitting mere popularization or repetition of earlier work. In this new and more specialized selection dealing with the problems and the psychology of women, I have followed a similar procedure, cutting to avoid repetition and redundancy without disturbing the author's intention or the continuity of her thought. The primary source of material has been the incomplete manuscript on the psychology of women referred to above, but I have not hesitated to draw on other relevant writings among the selected papers.

MAURICE R. GREEN

Foreword

I knew Clara Thompson over a period of many years
as a colleague, friend, and administrator. She played an
important role in the development of psychoanalysis in
the United States because the needs of psychoanalysis
and her personal qualities complemented each other in
a remarkable way.

Psychoanalysis, which is a theoretical system of dynamic psychology and at the same time a therapy for
mental disorders, has had a peculiar fate. Instead of
remaining a scientific discipline and a therapeutic art, it
developed a "movement." The apparent reasons for this
development were:

(1) The need to establish standards of training for
those who wanted to become psychoanalysts. This was
a particular problem for psychoanalysis, in contrast to
medicine for instance, because universities refused to
offer such training; thus private training centers had to
be established, and they had to develop their own
standards and training methods.

(2) The problem became aggravated by the general
hostility against psychoanalysis current among most
professionals until the late twenties combined with the
tendencies of some psychoanalysts to make concessions
to the currents of public opinion by softening and
emasculating Freud's theory. For these reasons Freud

and his early disciples felt compelled to establish not only strict criteria for training, but also to lay down rules concerning the legitimate application of the terms "psychoanalysis" and "psychoanalyst." In addition, and less explicitly, Freud and some of his pupils had aims which transcended theory and therapy. Freud was propelled by a sense of a mission to give man full knowledge of himself and thus to realize the aims of Enlightenment philosophy in a more profound and penetrating way.*

Such motivations for the formation of a psychoanalytic movement are understandable; however, they implied grave dangers. Once one tries to determine what is "legitimate" in theory, there are individuals and groups who are empowered to lay down the rules. This in turn leads to the formation of a bureaucracy in charge of the development of theory and therapy which tends to become a power apparatus precisely because it controls not only theory and therapy but the professional existence of those who practice psychoanalysis.

This is what happened to the psychoanalytic movement, with the result that a bureaucratic and often fanatical spirit took hold of the leadership of the movement, which tended to exclude psychoanalysts who held divergent or critical opinions. As a result, various groups of analysts declined to accept this situation and formed independent training groups and societies of their own. In this, and in other similar situations, the danger exists that in turn the leaders of such opposition groups develop into bureaucrats and show the same fanaticism which they previously combatted. If this danger is to be avoided, very special personalities are needed.

Clara Thompson was one of these rare persons who could take a leading role in the formation of an independent psychoanalytic group and continue to guide it. She was a thoroughly independent person, averse to rules and principles with which she did not agree; at the same time she did not endow her own theoretical prin-

* For the details of this thought cf. Erich Fromm, *Sigmund Freud's Mission* (New York: Harper & Row, 1959).

ciples with a halo that would make her fight all others. But while she was never a fanatic or one to intimidate others, it was one of her remarkable characteristics that she could not be intimidated. She acted according to her convictions, and she stood by her friends. No threat or bribery could move her to change her position. This integrity within and loyalty to friends made it possible for others to trust her and rely on her. She was a person with fine appreciation of theory and, at the same time, with excellent common sense. But beyond all this, she was a warm, devoted, and nurturant person. When she began to guide the William Alanson White Institute, she did so with a deep concern for her students and colleagues, with great patience, and with remarkable modesty. All these qualities made it possible for her to lead the institute without ever permitting it to become the center of a "school" in which one special theory was taught as the right and orthodox one.

This spirit, so characteristic of her, was also characteristic of her great teacher, Sándor Ferenczi. A gifted and brilliant analyst, he, too, was always ready to listen seriously to opinions that differed from his own. Clara Thompson continued his tradition, and it may be said without exaggeration that this objectivity, tolerance, and concern made it possible for the William Alanson White Institute to grow as an independent psychoanalytic institute and to avoid bureaucratic restrictions or fanatical claims that it represented the "one and true" theory.

This volume will impress the reader with the same qualities in the theoretical writings of Clara Thompson which I have tried to describe as characteristic of her personality.

ERICH FROMM

Biologic Aspects

Before any extensive study of the problems of womanhood in our society is undertaken, I shall attempt to state clearly the biologic facts which distinguish her from man. These fundamental differences exist and cannot be overlooked in any appraisal of her position in a given society. This statement seems so self-evident that it need not be made. Yet militant fighters for women's rights have tried to ignore or even deny this fact. In trying to show that a woman is just as good as a man, the tendency often has been to prove she is just like a man. Obviously, she is neither exactly like a man nor is she totally different. She shares many capacities with him but the difference remains.

The nature and extent of the biologic difference must in some respects inexorably assign her to a different role in life from the male. Of course, the most fundamental difference is the fact that she has different genitals and they have a different function. She also has breasts which are capable of producing milk. These are not only anatomic differences, but through the hormone productions of these organs, they have a far-reaching physiologic effect on the body, and some writers believe this also influences the emotional reactions and even the personality. Since many other factors influence the last two, the purely biologic influence is difficult to evaluate. Even the exact influence of the hormones on the body as well as on the emotions is found to vary widely among individuals. In general, the female has a voice of higher pitch than the male, she is smaller and more delicately built, her hips are broader, and she does not have and is not built to have the muscular strength of the male. She also does not have a beard—simply to mention some of the most outstanding differences. Margaret Mead reports that these secondary sexual differences are not uniform throughout the world. Among the Balinese, for example, the females approximate what we call the male type of build and the males approximate our female type of figure. Also in some races the male has very little beard. I do not believe hormone studies have been made on any typical examples of these other cultures; consequently, we cannot state how deep-seated the difference is. In our own society, we have as variations within the group the woman with the boyish build and the male with broad hips, as well as numerous other irregularities. It also has been observed that modern civilized man who no longer engages in such strenuous physical work as his ancestors shows less difference from the female in body structure than his primitive ancestors. This was observed in comparing skeletons. Whereas in primitive skeletons the sex is easily determined, the findings in examining the bones of modern man are often inconclusive. This conceivably is a variation due to changed occupation, since a great number of men no longer engage in strenuous physical labor. But whatever differences and changes occur in secondary sexual differences, two things remain constant in all races, i.e., women alone bear children and lactate.

It seems reasonable to assume that the hormonal differences between the two sexes have some effect on the way the one or the other copes with life. There is perhaps still some question whether differences affect attitudes and activities other than those specifically related to the sexual life.

Benedek and Rubenstein, in studying the relation of ovarian activity and psychodynamic processes, have

presented material to show that there is a definite relation between mood swings of aggressivity and passivity,
dependency attitudes and independence, and the differing hormone production of the various phases of the
menstrual cycle.* While the problems, with which each
woman has to cope, are the result of her personal
experiences, the way in which she copes with them, for
example, with aggressiveness or with depression and
resignation, according to these writers, is contingent
upon which hormone is dominating the picture in the
course of her four-week cycle. Other research workers
question whether such a strict correlation of attitudes
with hormone production is true in all cases. In short,
they have not obtained such uniform results as Benedek
and Rubenstein. Therefore it is not certain just how
much of this is purely organic effect. The way one feels
is certainly much influenced by the society in which one
lives, its customs, its attitudes toward work, education,
and sex. In addition, personal life experiences leave
their mark on the individual.

Certain physiologic activities are recognized by all
societies as belonging exclusively to the female. The
attitudes toward these activities may vary from culture
to culture. Menstruation, pregnancy, childbirth, lactation, and the menopause are universally recognized as
female experiences. There are records of a few males
who have under unusual circumstances lactated and
some who have had something approximating a menstrual cycle, even with bleeding from the nose or axilla,
for example. But this is not the usual run of male
behavior. More subtle and yet to some extent biologic
are the differences in sexual response of the two sexes.
Since the male has a penis and ejaculates and the
female has no penis and does not ejaculate, we can
assume, although we cannot know with certainty, that
there is a qualitative difference between the subjective
sexual experiences of the two sexes. It may be that this
has some influence on the general personality, although

* Therese Benedek and B. B. Rubenstein, *The Sexual Cycle in
Women* ("Psychosomatic Medicine Monographs," Vol. III, Washington, D.C.: National Research Council, 1942).

at this point it becomes increasingly difficult to separate biologic and cultural influences. Numerous studies of male castrates and hermaphrodites have not shown a predominance of homosexual tendencies or desires to be feminine in them; although one would expect if biology alone were the determining factor that those deprived of typical male organs would seek different types of emotional expression from the normal male. When it comes to actual sexual interests, it would seem that emotional factors and early life experiences are in the majority of cases more important than the biologic endowment; but the fact still remains that the female sexual response is qualitatively different from that of the male.

There seem to be some differences in the biologic development in the two sexes even in childhood. According to statistical studies, girls mature faster than boys. This is apparent very early and, in fact, seems to be the case up to and including puberty, which usually occurs in the girl about two years earlier than in the boy, at least in our society. From this point on, statistics seem to accord the greater achievement to the male. That is, when he catches up with the girl, he rapidly strides ahead of her in most types of development and achievement. Here again one would need extensive cross-cultural study to test the universality of this statement. In all societies, the child is educated so early in the customs by which he must live, and the attitude of adults toward male and female children is so distinctly different that much that seems evidence of a future male or female character must be acquired from the environment.

The difference in anatomy is usually discovered by most children between the ages of two and three if they have any opportunity to observe it. The fact that the genitals can be a source of pleasurable body sensation is also discovered very early. It is questionable whether we can call the feelings thus aroused sexual in any adult meaning of the word. Freud so assumed. He thought that early sexual sensations in the little girl centered around the clitoris and that vaginal sexual sensations developed only at puberty. It was his assumption that the girl child did not even discover her vagina until puberty. He rightly pointed to the fact that the clitoris is a source of satisfaction for the female; but there is evidence that many children also discover the vagina early and that they also derive pleasurable sensations from manipulating it. Masturbatory activity around the entrance of the vagina is especially frequently observed. It is my observation that when the vagina is early discovered as a pleasure zone, it frequently remains the most important source of pleasure throughout life. In fact there seem to be women who have never discovered the clitoris and who are not aware that they have such an organ. This does not preclude sensations from it adding to the total sexual satisfaction. Ford and Beach,* however, believe the clitoris is the most important organ for the production of orgasm, and they postulate the hypothesis that in female animals orgasm possibly does not take place because the clitoris is not stimulated because of the *a tergo* position assumed in coitus. I am not in a position to question their thesis about animals, but women patients have reported complete orgastic experience in coital positions where the clitoris could not have been stimulated. A few women are aware of rhythmic contractions of the vaginal walls during orgasm. It seems likely that in the human female at least there are two areas where the peak of sexual excitement may be experienced, the clitoris and vagina, and the relative importance as a source of stimulation of one or the other seems to vary with different women. It is doubtful whether this variation is due to actual physiologic differences. There is at least some evidence from the analysis of patients to support the thesis that early conditioning may place the emphasis on one or the other; thus, early vaginal experiences may make this the more important source of satisfaction. With many women the orgasm seems to arise from both organs, either simultaneously or it begins in the clitoris and

* Clellan S. Ford and Frank A. Beach, *Patterns of Sexual Behavior* (New York: Harper & Brothers, 1951), pp. 30 f.

passes to the vagina. At any rate, the fact that orgasm can rise from two centers and that it is not accompanied by ejaculation must make it a different type of physiologic experience from that of the male. I have wondered whether the experience of male castrates, as reported by Daniels and Tauber,* i.e., orgasm without ejaculation, is similar to the experience of the female. It would be interesting to know in what way these men found the experience before and after castration qualitatively different emotionally.

Culturally, we have been educated to think of women as having less sexual drive than men. On this basis, it was assumed that they could endure abstinence indefinitely. This was the rationalization for the double standard of sexual morality of the Victorian era. Observation of animals does not seem to confirm this, according to Ford and Beach. The sexual drive of the female in heat is insatiable. One female at that time can exhaust several males. Benedek's and Rubenstein's reports also show in women a periodic insistence on sexual activity, which, when frustrated, results in tension, irritability, and resentment. It seems that the sexual drive in women shows a more regular periodicity than in men, but it is no less insistent.

At the same time, it is more possible for a woman not to be aware of sexual tension as such than it is for a man. Since she is not aware of an erection (although the clitoris is capable of some degree of erection) and does not have an ejaculation, sexual need may be experienced merely as vague general tension. Girls may masturbate for years without experiencing orgasm or being aware that such a reaction is possible. Again the absence of tangible evidence, such as the male ejaculation, makes its discovery less certain. Nevertheless, many girls do discover orgasm; when it is once discovered, it becomes a regular part of sexual experience.

Another important aspect of a woman's sexual life is

* Edward S. Tauber, "Effects of Castration upon the Sexuality of the Adult Male," *Psychosomatic Medicine,* II (1940), 74–87; Edward S. Tauber and George E. Daniels, "Sex Hormones and Psychic Conflict, a Case Report," *Psychosomatic Medicine,* III (1941), 72–86.

the fact that the first coitus is usually a painful experience and results in a definite bodily alteration. The rupture of the hymen has usually been noted in some way in most cultures. For some, the act of defloration is ceremonially performed by a priest. In some, an older man, the father, the chief, or the lord of the manor has the right to the first coitus with a virgin. In our society virginity at the time of marriage has been considered very important. Thus the hymen has secondarily acquired great significance, and many emotional reactions to the fact of its existence or nonexistence are therefore due to cultural attitudes. However, perhaps, there is deep in the race such a thing as biologic virginal fear of coitus traceable to the hymen, and this may account for the picture frequently held by women of intercourse as an act of violence.

There seems to be more than one type of orgasm in the female. Some women have a sharp convulsive climax followed by relaxation and loss of sexual desire. Except for the absence of ejaculation, this type of experience seems to be very similar to that of the male. In contrast, many women report repeated orgasms during the period of a single coitus. Whatever these experiences are, they do not have the effect of complete discharge of tension at any one moment. Some women are not aware of any definite climaxes during coitus, yet find the experience pleasurable and relaxing. Some of these differences, especially the last mentioned, are often related to emotional difficulties or inhibitions; that is, the woman does not have orgasm completely because she cannot permit herself a sufficient degree of emotional freedom to give herself up unconditionally to the experience. When this is the case, there is a change in the type of orgasm in the course of analysis. All that one can say on the purely physiologic level is that women seem to be capable of varying degrees of orgasm, as well as orgasm originating in two different areas, and that the whole picture is overshadowed by psychogenic factors.[1]

[1] Notes and References, p. 179.

The first changes indicating the onset of puberty are signals in most cultures for a changed attitude toward both sexes. In the case of the girl, in many societies there are special ceremonies connected with the first menstruation. In all cultures beginning with the first menstruation the role of the female becomes definitely differentiated from that of the male. The biologic fact is that the periodic monthly cycle becomes established, and every four weeks the woman passes through various hormonal changes, which certainly have some effect on her emotional states. It is conceded by most observers that most women have a period of heightened sexual desire around the time of ovulation. Also a period of heightened sexual tension is frequent a day or two before the onset of menstruation. Benedek and Rubenstein report that, in the period before ovulation, women tend to be more aggressive. They are more self-assertive, and there is activity related to heterosexual desire. This they correlate with estrone production. After ovulation, they find the woman more passive, more receptive, and desirous of being loved. At that time another hormone is in the ascendancy—progesterone. As I have already said, these findings do not seem to be universally true of women. Other workers have found no constant correlation. It seems apparent that in some women these rhythms are more marked than in others, and psychogenic factors can greatly alter the picture. There are objective ways of determining when a woman ovulates. There is a change in body temperature. Also, vaginal smears indicate fairly accurately the various stages of the ovarian cycle. In addition, some women are aware of a definite sensation at the time of the rupture of the ovarian follicle. The general fact is that women have an approximate four-week hormonal cycle which determines to some varying extent their tensions, moods, and even at times their efficiency and energy.

Of course, all women are very much aware of menstruation. This plays an important role in every woman's life, both physiologically and psychologically. Physiologically, it is but one phase of the ovarian cycle, but in cases of infantile uterus or endocrine imbalance or malpositions of the uterus, it may be a painful experience and anticipated with dread. For women with these difficulties, it becomes an ever-present preoccupation hanging over them from month to month. For the normally developed woman the physical hazards of menstruation are minimal, and in our society, at least, it is looked on chiefly as an inconvenience or is in fact sometimes greeted with joy if the woman has feared she was pregnant when she did not wish to be. It can also be greeted with sorrow when the reverse is the case. There is still in our society some feeling of shame connected with menstruation. It is usually concealed from the opposite sex and great effort is made to disguise the odor. In primitive tribes the woman is often isolated during this period, and there are various superstitions concerning menstrual blood, such as that it is poisonous and that it ruins crops if a menstruating woman tills them. There has been some attempt to check on these beliefs, and there seems to be no conclusive evidence in favor of them. Especially during the Victorian era, it was thought women should be discouraged from physical activity during this period, and it was assumed that she would act as a semi-invalid at such a time. With the greater physical freedom and activity accorded girls today, there is much less tendency to make an event of menstruation. The average healthy girl does not often alter her plans because of it. In fact, some continue strenuous athletic activities during their periods, and there is a question whether this can have any unfavorable effect on the general health, although some physicians think so. Because menstruation is obvious and uncontestable evidence of femaleness, many neurotic attitudes become attached to it; many painful menstrual periods are not due to organic difficulties at all but to protests against being female. Also, the ovarian cycle is greatly influenced by all kinds of emotional stresses, such as grief and anxiety. Its psychogenic irregularities are not simply influenced by disturbances in the sexual sphere.

Another exclusively female biologic fact is pregnancy, and associated with it is labor and lactation. From the approximate age of fourteen to forty-five or fifty the possibility of pregnancy is a factor in the lives of all physically normal women. There are occasional sterile women who are otherwise healthy, and in our society (and some others) a woman may consciously choose not to have children or she may limit the number she chooses to have. Whatever happens or what she consciously does about it has an important effect on her life. In other words, for a woman, pregnancy must be reckoned with positively or negatively. The female organism is so constituted that pregnancy is its natural biologic goal and many women find in it the complete fulfillment of themselves. In these women one finds a physical blossoming and sense of well-being associated with pregnancy. The failure to have any children conceivably has some biologic and physiologic consequences even in women who think that failure to have children is their conscious preference. The attitude toward pregnancy, of course, becomes strongly conditioned culturally. But whatever the pressures, the fact of the possibility of pregnancy is some kind of factor in every woman's outlook in life. For an expanding culture where increase of population is needed, many children are desired. For societies where the struggle for existence is greater, limitation of progeny is the rule, and a woman must find other sources of self-fulfillment.

The physical experience of pregnancy itself cannot be ignored. The profound body changes have to be reckoned with and an adjustment to the situation must be made. This is undoubtedly easier of achievement when the pregnancy is greatly desired. Unwanted pregnancies with the attendant resentment are incorporated in the life of the woman with much more difficulty. There may also be physiologic difficulties not predominantly psychogenic, or at least where the psychogenic factors are so far removed from consciousness that insight into them is possible only after long analysis. For some women pregnancy seems to stimulate the body to its best function, while for others pregnancy is a physical burden, with an increase of any physical handicaps already in existence. In the latter case, the nine months are one long experience of discomfort.

Labor in the human is a more hazardous process than in animals. The great size of the human head makes its passage through the birth canal more difficult than is the case for the animal, except in certain over-bred animals such as the bulldog. However, the attitude of the woman toward labor plays a very important part in its difficulty or ease. Self-consciousness and shame about body functions, as well as fear of pain, make it more difficult for the woman to give herself up to the physiologic forces at work within her. In general, the less inhibited the woman, the less difficult the labor, except in definitely pathologic conditions, such as malformations of the pelvis or abnormalities in the child. In recent years there has been a "back to nature" movement among a small group of American women. They have chosen to go through labor without anesthesia. Some report definite satisfaction in this experience. There is a feeling of achievement, of being a part of a creative process. Two patients reported to me that the whole experience had an erotic value. One said that she experienced definite orgasm during the passage of the head through the birth canal. For most women, however, the pain is too great for any definite awareness of erotic satisfaction.

Lactation follows normally after childbirth; in primitive women it is accepted as a matter of course and continued for periods of varying length. This period of close intimacy of mother and newborn child is considered of great psychologic importance to the child. According to Sullivan, the child at this time experiences much through empathy with the mother. The American woman has been discouraged in nursing her child. Most obstetricians assume that the woman is more concerned in preserving the beauty of her breasts than in nursing her child, or that at least she is unwilling to have her freedom of movement restricted to the extent that nursing a child would require. At any rate there seems to be something in our American way of life which discourages a prolonged period of breast feeding;

so much so that even women who consciously wish to nurse their children have difficulty in producing enough milk.

A possible explanation of this is that when there is insufficient milk it is customary to give supplemental feedings. While these correct the immediate lack, they also tend to hasten the diminution of mother's milk, for the child when adequately fed has less need to work at the more arduous task of nursing, and thus the mammary glands receive less stimulation. Before the days of adequate methods of sterilization of milk, failure of the mother's milk was a calamity and the rearing of the child became much more hazardous. Today breast feeding is no longer essential to the physical welfare of the child. Consequently, the newborn infant may be turned over almost at once to the care of others. Many women do this—especially among those who must work. This denial of a biologic activity must have its effect on both mother and child. One is able to learn more about the reactions of the mother than of the child—the child's experience being entirely on a pre-verbal level, so that even in deep analysis one does not get memories of convincing authenticity about this period of life.

Whether the child is nursed or not, the care of the young infant is usually the responsibility of the mother, and in many ways this period is more consuming of her time, energy, and patience, more disrupting of her other interests, than even the period of pregnancy. As far as I know, there is no society which routinely turns over the care of the young to the male, although there are isolated examples of a male's becoming the mothering one. Judging from the observation of animals (and we must remember their behavior does not necessarily hold for the human), once nursing has been established, there is an instinctual drive in the mother to protect and care for the young. This apparently frequently only happens after the female's breasts are stimulated. Among some animals there is danger of the mother's eating her offspring at birth. In fact, in some species it is a marvel that enough survive to carry on the race.

Apparently the tendency to destroy the young disappears after breast feeding is established. This, of course, makes one wonder whether in the human there is less instinctual "mother love" when the child is not breast-fed. Obviously, this question cannot be answered for one can ask does the mother fail to nurse her child because she lacks instinctual drive or does she lack instinctual drive because it was not stimulated by nursing. And what of the woman who cannot nurse her child and yet has plenty of "mother love." In short, it is probable that the tendency of the human mother to be very responsible for the welfare of her child has more than purely instinctual roots, although one cannot rule out instinct as one of the factors.

Finally, one more biologic aspect of a woman's life differs from the male. Her period of reproductive capacity is more limited than his. By the age of fifty, the cyclic rhythm of a woman's reproductive capacity has ended for most women. A man's reproductive capacity tapers off more gradually, and men over seventy have been known to impregnate women. However, although a woman's reproductive capacity ends, her capacity for sexual enjoyment does not necessarily end. The menopause in our society is frequently accompanied by great emotional disturbance. Certain feelings have an organic basis. The great endocrine readjustment necessitated by the dropping out of some hormonal activity often occasions some discomfort, e.g., hot flashes. However, today the organic aspects of menopause discomfort can usually be pretty well controlled by the administration of hormones (although this must be done with care); by far the greatest hazards of the menopause are psychogenic or culturally induced, and these are not so simply dispelled by a few pills. A psychiatrist working in China reported to me that she had never seen a menopausal psychosis in a Chinese woman. This she attributed to the fact that in China the older woman has a secure and coveted position. Unlike the situation of older women in our society, she acquires an added dignity and power at this time. This would indicate that menopause disturbances are largely psychogenic.

Ford and Beach are of the opinion that in animals the female is more definitely dominated by her instinctual drives than the male. As proof of this, they cite the fact that in decerebrate cats, the female is able to go through her sexual activity without a cortex, but the male is no longer able to perform. I doubt if there are any statistics to show whether the female human is more dominated by instinct than the male. One must say it is within the realm of possibility. At least whatever instinctual drives still remain in the human are different in the two sexes. One of the concerns in this book is to what extent do the differing basic experiences affect a woman's outlook in life, her mental capacities, in short, the kind of contribution she has to make. Here we immediately come upon factors fully as powerful and fateful as biology.

Many other so-called biologic differences between men and women have been reported, such as that women do not create great works of art or that they are not as clever at mathematics. They have a stronger color sense, they have less need for physical activity, etc. These would constitute differences not directly connected with the genitals but presumably influenced by hormonal differences. However, cross-cultural studies have not been made. Therefore, there is not conclusive evidence that these differences are universally maintained, and one must concede that cultural factors have a powerful influence on these activities.

Psychoanalytic Theories

To psychoanalysis belongs the credit for the first intensive scientific study of the psychology of women. In the 1890's Freud greatly disturbed the Victorian world by announcing that it was not possible to ignore the sexual life of either sex without serious consequences. He came to this conclusion from the revelations of his patients. As a result of his findings, he dared to say that women also have sexual needs and desires and that the denial of these can produce neurosis. Since many patients' problems took them back to memories of their childhood, Freud presently became concerned with the sexual development of the child. His observations, based chiefly on the reminiscences of adult patients, have furnished some of the framework of child psychology. Since his early pronouncement, great numbers of children have been observed during their early years; many of Freud's hypotheses have been confirmed but others are more open to question, especially his conclusions about the sexual development of women. In fact he himself was not satisfied with his theories about female development.

Since the psychoanalytic theories about sexual development have permeated present-day thinking on the subject even more than most people realize, a review and critique of Freud's theory are important at this point. Freud's early observations applied more to the male than to the female child. He at first dismissed the female as having the same picture as the male in reverse. Thus the Oedipus complex, one of his earliest discoveries, is described as the little boy's desire to get rid of his father and sleep with his mother. The hostility and rivalry in relation to the father and the erotic interest in the mother were considered universal experiences in the development of the small child. The female child seemed to have a similar situation, with the parents reversed; the little girl had an erotic interest in her father and looked on her mother as the rival she would like to supplant. This simple contrast on further investigation proved to be unsatisfactory to Freud. The relation of children to their parents was much more complicated. Freud concluded that the Oedipus situation did not occur until sometime between the ages of three and five, and it became apparent to him that the relationship of children of either sex to at least one parent, the mothering one, had significance in his development before the Oedipus stage. As soon as Freud began to observe the emotional interactions of the earliest years, he concluded that there were important points of difference in the development of the two sexes.

The father, according to his observation, does not figure much in the life of the child before the age of three. The first relationship is one of oral dependency upon the mother. The newborn infant is completely helpless and must depend upon someone for everything. It is thought that he at first is not aware of himself as something separate from his environment. The mothering one furnishes a protecting medium which the child does not differentiate from himself and to which he relates predominantly through his mouth. At this stage both sexes have the same type of relationship to the mother, and the activity which dominates the picture is nursing. Freud did not stress other aspects of this earliest relationship, such as closeness to the mother's body, but this is probably also an important experience for the newborn. Although the behavior of both male and female child at this stage is similar actually they have started along different paths, for the male child is relating to the opposite sex. In other words, he is already developing along the lines of his ultimate object choice, while the girl child has her first relationship with a member of her own sex. Another fact is that the mother, even at this stage, may feel differently toward a child of one sex than toward one of the other. A boy may be especially desired at one time and a girl at another. Freud thought that a woman found her greatest fulfillment in producing a male child. Certainly in a patriarchal culture this is often a very important achievement and a cause for special rejoicing in the family. The mother is somehow usually given the credit for bringing this about although obviously she has no conscious control over the matter.

The difference in sex does not yet figure as such, according to Freud, in the second stage of development, called by him the anal stage. At this time he stated that the child's innate tendencies to activity or passivity may become more apparent, although he did not stress the difference as necessarily being linked to sex. His assumption, however, was that the male child is likely to tend more toward an active, rebellious, even sadistic attitude, while the little girl begins to show her tendency to be obedient, compliant, and masochistic. A passive attitude in a male at this stage he believed might foreshadow homosexual development. The central point of this period of development is the problem of toilet training. This Freud saw as a biologic stage with erotic satisfactions in the anal region. Cross-cultural anthropologic studies show that this period has wide variations, both as to time of appearance and the nature of the child's reaction depending upon the parental attitudes, culturally conditioned, toward control of the products of excretion. In some cultures, early cleanliness in this respect is not at all important. In our own, however, there is great emphasis on toilet training, and it is one of the points where the child first feels a clash between his own will and that of his parents. The tendency toward compliance in girls and rebellion in boys, insofar as it is true, may not be due to biologic differences but to different attitudes on the part of parents toward the two sexes. Thus many mothers are more permissive toward their sons and more concerned in making their daughters "little ladies." However, in some children a pronounced maleness or femaleness seems apparent very early and some of the characteristic behavior may be innate.

The next stage of development, occurring between the ages of two and one-half and three, termed by Freud the phallic stage, was thought to be a period of great significance in the differentiation of the ways of life of the two sexes. It was thought that at this time both little girls and little boys received a shock. This is the period of discovery of the genitals, and it is at this point that girls discover that they lack something and boys discover that there are people who have "lost" the precious organ. This presumably produces anxiety in both sexes. If the boy had ever been threatened with having his penis cut off because of masturbation, this discovery about girls' anatomy would seem to prove that such really could take place. Girls' reasoning similarly must conclude that they have already been punished and can only envy their luckier brothers. It was believed that the little girl was as yet unaware of her vagina, that she perceived her state as being without a penis rather than as a positive state of difference, i.e., "You have a penis and I have a vagina." Thus Freud concluded that it is at this period that the boy develops castration fear and the girl penis envy. For a time both try to evade the tragic realization by thinking the little girl's clitoris will grow. Eventually this hope is abandoned. Since the absence of a penis is equated with punishment, for a long time children continue to think that the mother has a penis. This whole idea seems to be truer of the thinking of little boys than of little girls. Occasionally there is a patient who recalls having thought that she once had a penis and lost it. In my experience, this is an exceptional case with definite special conditioning factors. Many women who recall having envied their brother's possession of a penis at this stage do not recall any feeling that they had lost anything or that their lot was a punishment.

From direct observation of children, this concern with penis or no penis around the age of two or three is corroborated. Competitive experimental urination leaves the girl defeated. The old joke about the little girl who on observing her brother's skill at urinating said, "How practical to have on picnics," is a valid bit of child psychology. The question is whether the discovery is necessarily traumatic and whether it need produce any lasting envy or anxiety. (For a more detailed discussion, see pp. 73–78, "Penis Envy"—Ed.)

Not only is the phallic phase of development the period of anatomic sexual discoveries but, according to Freud, at this period the child's attitude toward the mother changes. Up to this point the prevailing reaction is one of dependence and passivity. The mother is the active one. Now both boy and girl assume an aggressive attitude toward the mother. In the boy this merges easily into the Oedipus phase of erotic interest in her, but it is at this point that the girl begins to feel frustrated. Freud terms this brief period of phallic aggressiveness on the part of the girl her positive Oedipus phase. In short, her first active relationship is to the mother. Eventually her lack of a penis (supposedly thought of as castration) forces her to relinquish the relation to the mother. She blames her mother for the loss of the organ of aggression and the relation is broken in hostility. She is then supposed to turn to the father from whom she hopes she will receive a baby as a consolation for her lost penis. Thus the little girl begins her Oedipus phase of development (in later Freudian theory called the passive Oedipus). As time goes on the hoped-for baby does not appear, and she gradually relinquishes her interest in the father, but she never entirely turns away from him, and her interest in him is revived again at puberty.

This theoretical construction of the girl's relation to her mother seems to me debatable. That children become more aggressive as they gain confidence in their ability to do things for themselves is a fact. It is a trying period for parents, especially mothers who must succeed in maintaining enough control to make life in the home bearable. So the mother at this time must seem to the child to be the frustrating one, and I suspect that both sexes have some pretty hostile feelings for her, and it is at this point that the child begins to try to play one parent against the other and thus get what he wants.

At the end of the Oedipus phase, Freud assumes that there is a latency period during which interest in sexual activity dies down. One reason for this is that the child has learned all that he can on the subject until the maturation of his sexual organs at puberty. The boy also turns away from interest in sex for another reason, according to Freud. His sexual interest in his mother has created a conflict in his attitude toward his father. He looks upon his father as a rival and wishes to have him out of the way. At the same time he admires his father and desires his approval. Fearing the loss of the father's love, and also fearing that the father will punish him, he renounces his sexual interest in the mother and tries to identify with his father's attitude toward him. In everyday language, he develops a conscience. It is at this point that the little girl's genitals serve as a potent reminder of the type of punishment which would fit his crime. He therefore gives up sexual interests because of fear of castration. The girl, since she is already castrated, according to Freud, has not such a strong need to turn away from her love for her father. Freud assumed that the greater independence and stronger conscience of the boy child was due to this sharp break, whereas girls never develop such strong convictions and principles as boys. For a woman, the need to be loved is supposed to be so great that she tends to adopt the standards and beliefs of any man who loves her. In Freud's words, she does not develop a strong superego of her own. He and his immediate followers were of the opinion that for this reason women are not capable of the same degree of moral integrity as men. They are likely to echo the convictions of the most recent man influencing their lives. In so far as this can be observed in women, it is questionable whether it has any connection with sexual differences per se. It is a characteristic of people in an inferior position, where they are dependent upon the whims and authority of a more powerful one, to try to get along with that person, often to the extent of espousing his interests and convictions or at least seeming to do so. In Victorian days and even later in middle-class European society, women were usually in this position in relation to their fathers and husbands. The same lack of moral strength, however, can be ovserved in men in dependent positions.

It has been questioned whether the latency period is a fact. It is certainly not found in some cultures and is by no means universal in our own society. Complete suppression of sexual interest and curiosity between the ages of six and ten would probably occur only when the child has been severely frightened concerning his interest. In most cases the interest is less intense than it is to become with the beginning of prepuberty changes. Many new activities appear in the so-called latency period, and these may detract from the interest in body function. This is the time when the child first begins to know the world outside the home. The problems of socialization may become temporarily very absorbing. With prepuberty changes, the attention is again drawn to one's own body and its functions. Uninhibited girls eagerly compare the growth of their breasts. The first pubic hairs are also noted with curiosity, and finally, for the girl who has developed without grave personality damage, menstruation is an achievement about which she is proud.

However, Freud saw the onset of puberty as a difficult time for the girl. Since he believed that the vagina and its sensations were not discovered by the girl in childhood and that her sole source of pleasure and sexual interest was in her clitoris, he believed that the girl must undergo a major readjustment at puberty. With the onset of menstruation, she must discover her vagina and its function and renounce her clitoris and her boyish interests and tendencies. This, Freud said, is very difficult to achieve, especially if the girl suffered from strong penis envy. With the acceptance of the vagina, Freud assumed the girl accepts her passive role in life. Here again Freud was talking about middle-class Victorian women who indeed did have to accept a grave limitation of their activities at puberty. Up to that point, they had played with boys, often had similar education and freedom of activity. With the onset of menstruation, a girl's life was changed. Her freedom became markedly curtailed. She might no longer be openly and frankly friendly with boys. Further education was discouraged. In addition to the bewilderment occasioned by the new experience of puberty, she must develop an artificial shyness, pretend to be helpless, and so on. Much of this has changed in the last fifty years, and adolescents today have fewer cultural obstructions to cope with. However, since marriage is long delayed in our society, adolescence is teeming with storm and stress for both sexes, who have to learn to cope with an adult sexual drive in a culture which forbids its fulfillment or at least enforces penalties on any fulfillment which results in pregnancy. Because the female must pay the penalty for illegitimate pregnancy, most parents still supervise a girl's activities after puberty more carefully than they do a boy's.

On the basis of Freud's theory, Helene Deutsch has made further studies of the sexual life of woman. According to her, the occurrence of menstruation at puberty is traumatic in that it revives the old idea of castration. She places the emphasis on the appearance of blood. It is true that girls who have not been prepared for its appearance often react to its onset with the idea that they must have hurt themselves. This, it seems to me, is the result of an unfortunate cultural attitude.

In my opinion, menstruation would have the traumatic significance of castration only when it is a signal for a drastic discrimination against a girl's former activities. Otherwise, many girls today are proud of achieving it. It can be looked upon as a kind of initiation into a bigger, more important life. Some of the menstruation ceremonies of primitive people seem to have this significance. However, Deutsch further states that menstruation throughout the years has a certain traumatic quality in that it represents the fact that one is not pregnant, which she affirms is always experienced as a disappointment. This is certainly true of women who desire pregnancy, but I have the impression that Deutsch considers the desire for pregnancy a constant unconscious longing based on instinct need, no matter how great the woman's conscious negation of the desire is. I believe there is much truth in this and that at some period in every woman's life she experiences a longing for the complete fulfillment of her biological destiny. Whether a woman who has already had several children continues to feel frustrated at the appearance of each menstrual period is more open to question. At least the wish for pregnancy is very far from consciousness in such a case.

Deutsch also suggests that the woman partially consoles herself for lack of a penis by identification with the partner's pleasure in his penis. Ferenczi went even further with this idea and was of the opinion that the woman's chief pleasure in the sexual act was due to identification with the male. He thought her pleasure was entirely in his orgasm. This I think would be the case only of frigid women or partially frigid women. As I shall discuss later, I believe the woman's pleasure in orgasm is due to her own experience which has its own validity.

Deutsch further thinks of the woman's satisfaction as left incomplete after coitus. With the man, the single act is complete in itself, but for the woman sexual expression takes place in two parts. The act of coitus is merely the receiving aspect. The process is only completed by parturition which contains a pleasurable orgastic quality largely masochistic in nature. It has been suggested that woman's greater need for permanency in a sexual relationship may be due to this fact. She does not often succeed in taking sexual experiences casually. She has a tendency to want to bind the man. It is possible that the ever-present possibility of pregnancy has built a deep biologic need for continuity of a relationship into woman's nature. She may feel that she has received a very special gift from the man which ties her to him, while the man thinks of his semen as something discarded and having no further interest for him. One must question whether this attitude in women is true in all cultures. In matriarchies, and in communities having group marriages, women have *seemed* not to need this continuity, and we know that in our society other factors contribute to it. Certainly for the great majority of women there is still no financial security comparable to that of marriage, and socially a woman alone is at a disadvantage. These are very real factors in her craving for permanency. However, it is a fact that many pregnant women find real satisfaction in the thought that they have a gift from the mate constantly with them—if they love the mate. It also may produce genuine distress if they do not love the impregnator.

Another aspect of the Freudian theory is that women are incapable of object love. With the renunciation of her clitoris, she supposedly gives up the active conquering aim of seeking an object, and henceforth cannot love but only can permit herself to be loved. This is supposed to stem from the disappointment of not being able to win the mother because the girl has no penis. Thus she is condemned to lifelong inability to love, certainly a dubious concept. Even while postulating this, psychoanalysts continue to talk of mother love. They get around this by saying love of the child is really love of part of herself and therefore not true object love. In my experience, there is much evidence to show that the inability to love is not sex-limited but is found in those who have never been loved in childhood. While it may be true that a mother often gives more love to her son than to her daughter, and thus the daughter might more often be unloved in childhood, this is by no means a universal finding; even when a child is not loved by the mother, she may receive love from the father, nurse, grandmother, or someone. The absence of any loving relationship in childhood invariably produces serious personality damage in either sex. Perhaps there are actually fewer women capable of love than men but I doubt it.

While there are questionable aspects to Freud's theories about women, it is important to remember that no one else has as yet presented anything comparable in detail and specificity to his contribution. In fact, most observations of significance stem from Freud's thinking, even when they contradict it.

There seems to me to be a particularly basic fallacy in his theory, although many of his observations are empirically correct, and that is the idea that a woman is essentially a castrated male. She is supposed to have started life with a boyish outlook which necessitated a difficult reorientation at puberty and which condemns her to a lifelong envy of the male. Many facts which led to this conclusion are the product of cultural attitudes and a woman's psychology with all its problems is something in its own right and not merely a negation of maleness.

Childhood

When a child is born, all too frequently a boy or a girl is hopefully awaited. If the child turns out to be the "wrong" sex the parents are markedly disappointed. The reasons for preferring one or the other vary greatly. There is the patriarchal consideration that a man wants a son to carry on his name and perhaps his business, or, especially in America, that he may have the advantages which the father lacked. Or a girl may be desired because there already is a son or sons. Whatever the prenatal attitude toward the sex of the child, from birth on the actual sex subtly influences the reactions of the significant adults toward the baby. One woman who had always been somewhat militant in her insistence on the equality of men and women found to her amazement that her attitude toward her girl baby was different from the way she had felt about her sons. "In spite of myself, I feel more protective of her," she said. In short, whether we have consciously thought about it much or not, most of us have a collection of attitudes toward the female which are different from those we have toward the male. Some of these attitudes make sense in terms of biology and physiology but a great many of them are cultural stereotypes.

Freud was of the opinion that the boy outgrew the Oedipus phase more completely than the girl. He offered as a theoretical explanation the idea that the boy's incestuous interest in his mother roused his castration fears and that he presently renounced his interest in her because of this fear. The little girl, on the other hand, Freud felt, had no incentive for giving up her attachment to the father since she had no penis to lose. An alternative explanation to Freud's may lie in the fact that in the average home there is more tendency to be protective of girls than of boys. Boys are encouraged to find their way, to do things on their own, and fight their own battles. Girls tend to remain under parental protection longer and more completely than boys, and there is much less encouragement in independence. Therefore, girls tend to keep their early ties to the parents longer than boys. In the Victorian era a girl might very well remain attached to her father until she transferred the same dependency to her husband.

It is probable that small children when left to their own devices play equally well with either sex. But from the age of six on there is more and more tendency to distinguish between boys and girls. As puberty approaches the feeling of difference increases. Since girls usually mature a year or two before boys, the chasm between one-time playmates widens, and a sense of mystery deepens.

All of this sense of difference is usually reinforced by various rules, which are more stringent as they apply to girls. Unless there has been serious traumatic experience, by the age of twelve a girl is well on the way to becoming a woman of our particular social order.

A period of close association with one's own sex usually begins a year or so before puberty and extends into the early part of adolescence. An increasing need for intimacy at this time is responsible for the first close friendships. Often there are groups of girls who may call themselves a club or may just get together. They often have a secret language or exchange secrets. The beginning puberty changes in their bodies are a source of mutual interest, and information and misinformation about sex are frequent topics. One group of grammar-school girls met from time to time to inspect the prog-

ress of growth of each other's pubic and axillary hair;
later the growing breasts were subjects for comparison.
This displays an essentially healthy curiosity in the dra-
matic changes of bodily development. Of course mis-
informed groups can succeed in frightening each other
quite severely.

The intimacy between two people of the same sex
is a very important event. As Sullivan has pointed
out,* sometime between the ages of nine and twelve the
capacity for love develops. Prior to this time what the
parents call love in the child has been heavily colored
by dependency. At this point, however, the capacity to
care about what happens to another person appears—
her happiness is your happiness and her sorrow your
concern. As the sexual drive begins to mature, little-
understood emotions emerge toward boys. There is excitement, self-consciousness, a feeling of awkwardness,
and sometimes, defensively, a feeling of contempt for
the boys. The changes in the body and these feelings
about boys are often discussed in the intimate relationships between girl friends. Sexual experimentation with
each other also occurs, and many a parent becomes
concerned that she has a budding homosexual on her
hands. The healthy girl moves on from this, however,
to an interest in the opposite sex. If a girl reaches
adolescence having acquired a capacity for healthy companionship with her own sex, she is well on the road to
emotional maturity. Those who have not achieved such
preadolescent intimacy will come to grief in trying to
negotiate the more difficult step of heterosexual intimacy.

* Harry Stack Sullivan, *The Interpersonal Theory of Psychiatry*
(New York: W. W. Norton, 1953), pp. 245–262.

Adolescence

The onset of adolescence is marked in both sexes by a physiologic event, the beginning of the functioning of the sexual organs. Around this event in all cultures has collected an impressive number of attitudes, customs, and even, in many cases, rituals. From the onset of puberty every young person finds himself in a new situation.

Even in the best of situations the maturing of the lust dynamism, the last of our biologic dynamisms, creates complications in our society. Up to this point the child has been encouraged to exercise his powers as they develop. The mastery of the anal sphincter brings rewards of approval and admiration. The child's first steps and first words produce occasions for rejoicing. It is quite otherwise with the maturing of the sexual function. One of the most complex and powerful forces within us is subjected from its onset to stringent social regulations. In fact, in our society this amounts practically to prohibiting the exercise of this new function for many years. This attitude prompted Sullivan to call us "the most sex-ridden people of whom I have any knowledge." In other words, the necessity for rigid control of the powerful lust drive means that it is more or less ever-present in our thoughts, especially of the adolescent. All of which contributes to the fact that with us adolescence is a period of storm and stress.

In girls the actual physiologic demands are usually less overt than in boys. There are no erections or ejaculations insistently forcing sexual needs into consciousness. However, the periodic appearance of menstruation makes complete ignoring of the genitals impossible. Instead of the more focused and acute feelings of lust experienced by boys, the girl finds herself unexpectedly tense, irritable, and longing for love in a vague way.

But the adolescent girl must not only cope with the natural forces within, she must also learn to make this new part of herself conform to the standards of her social order. Prohibitions have been stronger for the female and punishment for violation of the rules more severe.

World War I introduced women into industry on a big scale and the sexual revolution began. The emancipation of women from their sexual inhibitions made the old control of the adolescent more difficult. Necking, petting, and all degrees of sexual intimacy, often in cars by the roadside, became the rule of the day. The change came too rapidly to be reasonably assimilated. Whereas, before, a sexual experience in adolescence was a disgrace, in the 1920's sexual activity among high-school girls was very frequent. In fact, among some groups, you weren't properly initiated into adolescence unless you had tried it. It was part of a general rebellion and demand for equal rights. "What a man can do I can do" was the slogan, and this applied to sex as well as to work or career. In the 1930's there was some swing of the pendulum back to a more conservative standard in sex, but there are still great discrepancies in the attitudes of different communities, and in different social groups in the same community, as to what constitutes socially acceptable sexual behavior in adolescents.

* * *

Although there are problems arising from the present attitude of excessive permissiveness there are positive gains also. Sex today is something that can be talked about. It is possible for the adolescent to get accurate information. Most preadolescents today do not look forward with fear to the onset of menstruation.

The greater frequency of sexual activity does not mean that our adolescents are necessarily free from inhibition. Just as girls in the past did not succumb to sexual overtures for fear of social disapproval, many today undertake sexual activity for social approval. Promiscuity is mistaken for freedom. Sex becomes a commodity, useful in buying a boy's attention or in buying popularity. Often the girl is frigid, thereby testifying to the fact that the experience is not genuine for her. In short, our adolescents have not reached the simple acceptance of sexuality that they are seeking. In attempting to be uninhibited they have for the most part oversimplified and devalued the situation.

Sex still remains in the human an important expression of intimacy. Its performance can express all types of relatedness from the most satisfying to the most hateful. We have seen that in preadolescence the young boy or girl has the possibility for the first time to care in an unselfish way about the happiness of another person. It remains for adolescence to present the next step, the relating of this to the sexual drive. This was difficult to do when sex was considered something dirty or evil. It is equally difficult to do when sex has become a commodity. Hence the adolescent girl today can become as confused about the real importance of sex in her life as her grandmother did, although the emphasis is different. Nevertheless, the greater sexual frankness of the present generation offers a less constricting background for growth to the girl who is healthy enough psychically to be able to utilize it.

* * *

The period of adolescence . . . presents these problems to be mastered—coming to some terms with the

sexual drive, assimilating sex to a significant relationship with another person, the struggle for independence
from the parents, and at least some preliminary deci-
sions about the future life plan. This latter decision can
still be altered in a woman's twenties unless some relatively irrevocable decision has been made—such as
marriage or an early breaking-off of education.

Whether a person comes to these important new
experiences with confidence or dread depends to a great
extent on what has happened in childhood. Certainly
the girl who has not succeeded in making an intimate
friend of another girl, who never became one of a
group, is usually even more appalled at the necessity of
being successful with boys. The girl who has never felt
secure in the home finds the struggle away from home
more terrifying.

On the other hand, in adolescence there is often a
tightening of the vested interests each parent has in the
child. The "good" animal mother lets her offspring go
as soon as they can fend for themselves. In fact she
devotes her energies to making them independent. The
human mother too often has personal stakes in her
children's dependence on her. She views their leaving
the home nest with alarm because of the anticipated
emptiness of her own life. This problem is of course
greatly multiplied when the mother is a widow or es-
tranged from her husband. Then she may try to enter
the social life of her children, appropriating her son for
herself, competing with the girls of his own age, or
openly competing with her daughter for the attentions
of the young men. Such a woman has certain advantages over her inexperienced adolescent competitors,
and she is usually not sufficiently old to be physically
unattractive. The children of such a mother usually have
already been made sufficiently helpless before adolescence so that they are unable to cope with this new
frustration of their development. In fact, it is not unusual to find the daughter of an attractive competitive
mother playing down her own feminine charm, dressing
unattractively, or insisting on being tomboyish. Such a

situation can be one of the factors contributing to overt homosexuality in the daughter.

Another type of mother-daughter situation is seen less frequently today. This is the case where the mother has loathed her sexual experiences; she feels the lot of women is bitter and has succeeded in frightening her daughter with pictures either openly described or implicitly conveyed of the grim fate of women. Such young women, more frequently seen two generations ago, do not try to make contact with the opposite sex and often devote their whole lives to their mothers. One can say that they do not even achieve a homosexual level of development. They remain unawakened, asexual, the dutiful attendants of their mothers.

Fathers, as described earlier, also often have a problem with their relation to adolescent daughters. The young girl just blossoming into womanhood is an attractive sight to anyone. Especially if the girl resembles her mother, memories of past years are activated, and the father finds the company of his daughter very pleasing. All of this is good for the girl up to a point; that is, it is good for her self-esteem to know that her father finds her attractive—it helps her accept her womanhood; but the father may become too possessive at this point. He may become jealous of any young man who appears . . . no one is good enough for his girl, and indeed a young man may find it difficult to compete with an experienced older man. Society looks more indulgently on a father's possessiveness of his daughter than on a mother's possessiveness of her son. One factor in this may be the fact that for an older man to be attractive to a younger woman is not considered incongruous, whereas an older woman interested in a younger man is somewhat freakish. Another reason why a father's possessive attitude toward his daughter is not frowned on is, as has been stated, that girls are not expected to be entirely on their own. Thus the young girl can bask in her father's adoration with full social approval, whereas the adolescent boy tied to his mother is considered a mama's boy.

Another type of father is more of a problem to his

adolescent daughter. This is the father who, perhaps because of his own repressed sexual interest in the girl, is suspicious of any interest she shows in the opposite sex. He is constantly worrying lest she get into sexual difficulties, he believes "the worst" of her, and may resort to very annoying spying activities or open accusations of immorality. Unlike the first father described, he does not build up the girl's self-esteem by his interest in her because he denies and abhors his own attraction to her. Such girls do in fact often become promiscuous. One finds in analysis that this is often more than simple rebellion. The girl has actually unconsciously incorporated into her own self-image her father's evaluation of her and proceeds to live it out.

The father who is indifferent to his daughter presents a different type of problem to her attempts at emancipation. She has probably had the same difficulty with him throughout childhood, but in adolescence the results of the indifference become more apparent. Two general types of solution often appear. She may devote all her energies to being seductive, thus trying to deny her father's indifference by proving that every other man is crazy about her. This usually does not work. No amount of popularity can give her the feeling of personal worth as a woman. The other solution is even more obviously a defeated one. She does not have the courage to try to attract a boy. She, too, like the girl with the competitive mother, may show no interest in personal appearance and may be drawn toward homosexuality.

Then there is the situation where the mother is competitive with the daughter for the father's love. In her search for contact with the other sex the girl may then be attracted only to men in some way belonging to other women. To win a man away from someone else becomes of paramount importance. Needless to say, as soon as she has won, the man may no longer be interesting to her. The other extreme of reaction is the girl who tries to conceal her competition by making herself unattractive in order to assuage the mother's jealousy. Underneath she may know or fantasy that she is the one preferred by her father; but because she has to conceal her attractiveness, it does not make for success with boys of her own age. To be sure there are differing degrees of playing the inconspicuous role, some of which can be successful in winning popularity with her compeers.

It would be impossible to name all of the possible combinations of parent-daughter reactions which complicate a girl's first steps away from the childhood ties. I have shown here that the problems of the parents play a conspicuous role in the process.

* * *

The transition from childhood and preadolescence to adulthood is eventually made through these stormy years of adolescence, but for the emotionally disturbed the teen years constitute one of the most hazardous periods of development. Schizophrenia often develops at this time. Various milder personality disorders also tend to become more clearly apparent. Some settle for a permanent preadolescent state in which intimacy with another person plays no part. Although such women may eventually marry, marriage then is only doing the correct thing, and love in such a marriage is at most rudimentary. However, much of what passes in our social order for adulthood proves on close scrutiny to be merely prolonged adolescence.

Psychopathology of Adolescence

Menstruation, in itself a normal function, frequently plays a very important role in psychopathology. As a normal function, it should create very little disturbance in a girl's life, but as a symbol of sex and womanhood it attracts unto itself pathologic attitudes and symptom formations. To the occasional girl with an infantile uterus or some malformation, the onset of menstruation actually initiates a life of periodic invalidism, which materially complicates her total situation. But this is by no means the usual situation. Menstruation has earned the nickname of "being unwell" and the "curse" for quite other reasons. The actual discomfort of a large number of girls during the menstrual period is very great, but it is to a surprising degree due to psychic causes. This discomfort varies greatly in individuals and also, in the same individual, at different times, quite different symptoms appear. Increased irritability, emotional instability, and slight loss of energy are very common. Actual malaise, severe pain, headaches, nausea, vomiting, and complete prostration may occur without demonstrable organic cause. Certainly, very often these symptoms are conversion phenomena, i.e., expressions in somatic symptoms of emotional states. Menstruation is a peculiarly suitable focus for neurotic manifestations, because it pertains to the sexual life and

52

to being a woman. If sex is associated in the girl's mind with disgust, menstruation as its symbol is disgusting. If a girl has a very strong feeling of revolt at being a woman, an attitude which occurs rather frequently, she resents menstruation. Psychoanalysis of menstrual nausea, headaches, and cramps often reveals such factors to be contributing to their causation. A wealth of superstition has been built up around menstruation and it is generally looked upon as a period of legitimate partial invalidism. This fact is used to the utmost by certain types of girls and women. This use of the menstrual period may vary all the way from conscious malingering, e.g., the girl who takes a day or two off from work each month on the plea of cramps, when she suffers never a pain—to the actual, although psychically determined, incapacitation of the woman who unconsciously hails this time as a period when she can regress to invalidism and be mothered. The latter situation is usually an indication of something wrong in the sexual life of these individuals.

Not only does menstruation attract to itself conversion symptoms because of its relation to sex and being a woman, but because of its importance in determining pregnancy, it may also become the focus of morbid fears. It is perhaps well to consider here some of the events which become associated fairly frequently with menstruation. Practically all mothers, even those most averse to any mention of sexual matters to their daughters, feel it their duty to give some information about menstruation. The self-conscious, sexually unoriented woman—and this description applies to a shockingly large number of mothers in our civilization—finds this occasion a real ordeal and may actually postpone the interview with daughter until menstruation actually appears. When such a mother attempts to do her duty, the daughter gets anything but benefit from the encounter. With the average girl, the information has already been acquired elsewhere. Nevertheless, the situation is extremely unpleasant—the girl reacts to her mother's embarrassment and this becomes associated in her mind as an unpleasantness relating to menstruation. Then some mothers take this opportunity to fortify their daughter's morals. A patient reports the following experience when her mother introduced her to the facts about menstruation. The mother said, "Now you must be careful for you can become pregnant and, if you ever do, I'll kill you. I won't have any disgrace around here." Even less harsh mothers manage to convey the same sentiment in milder terms. So menstruation is likely to become connected with the idea "I'm likely to do terrible things which will disgrace me for life." This idea, plus the actual fact that absence of menstruation is one of the signs of pregnancy, facilitates the development of morbid concern about the menses. Irregular menses often throw the young girl and her mother into a panic. The mother sees the girl with infrequent menses developing tuberculosis or "going into a decline." She sees the girl with too frequent menstruation dying of anemia or requiring surgical intervention. The girl is dragged to doctors. On the girl's part, the irregularities of the early months of menstruation form a basis for various fears. (It is even likely that the emotional states may actually influence the regularity of the menses.) At any rate, in some cases early childhood notions of impregnation by kissing or touching are revived, especially among the inadequately informed. Too frequent menstruation, on the other hand, is often connected in the girl's mind with fear that she has hurt herself by masturbation. Fairly often, also, one gets the history that a girl feared she had brought on her menstruation prematurely by masturbation. I have found this worry several times in girls where menstruation began at eleven. We are obviously dealing here with very complex situations involving the interaction of emotional factors to somatic conditions and it is not always easy to trace cause to effect. Suffice it to say therefore that menstrual difficulties are often closely connected with important disturbances of the total personality.

Aside from the very definite fact of menstruation, the subject of sex in general and especially the consciousness of its instinctual drives is much less clearly understood by girls than boys. Every physician who has had experience in taking sex histories from married women will corroborate the fact that very frequently women who have been engaging in a supposedly normal sexual life for years not only have never had orgasm, but have not even known that such an experience belonged to the sexual life of woman. Thus we find sexual sensations much vaguer and much less consciously realized in girls than in boys. This makes the significance of masturbation somewhat different. One often finds among the laity, and even among some physicians, a superstition that girls do not masturbate. Because of this attitude girls are less often the victims of quack literature, and they less often fall into the hands of reformers who impress them with the dangers of masturbation. It is perfectly possible for a girl to go through the adolescent masturbation period almost unaware that it is taking place. This is especially true when there is no actual manipulation of the genitals as, for example, when pleasurable sensations are obtained by pressing the thighs together. An extreme example is that of a woman with a very strong religious attitude, given to intense religious experiences. She was frigid with her husband and for many years was accustomed to pressing her thighs together when thinking some exalted thought about God. There would ensue a very distinct bodily thrill which she thought of as religious ecstasy and did not associate with sex until later, when a psychotic illness and subsequent analytic work made the nature of the feeling clear to her.

However, the fact that the situation is often not clearly conscious does not mean that it is always without conflict by any means. Some echo of childhood warnings and threats may contribute to a vague sense of guilt about a bodily feeling that isn't quite right. When these half-conscious masturbators do worry about themselves it is often not at all clear to them what they worry about. They may complain of feeling self-conscious, of blushing, of fatigue. They may worry about leucorrhea. When these symptoms are treated without understanding of the underlying cause the actual condition may be aggravated, e.g., increased periods

of rest for the abnormally tired adolescent simply
throws the opportunity for increased daydreaming in
her way. If she already has conflict about it increased
opportunity does not diminish the conflict. Similarly,
local treatment for leucorrhea psychogenically determined does not diminish the conflict already existing,
but adds the pleasure of local stimulation as a new
thing to have conflict about. Thus in a patient, a young
woman already heavily burdened with guilt feelings
about sexual fantasies, the prescribing of a douche pre-
cipitated acute panic with fears of contamination.

It would seem that in general the situation is something like this in adolescence. In the individual not
heavily emotionally handicapped who eventually works
her way through to adulthood a period of masturbation
may occur without conflict—it may or may not be
conscious—the fact that girls in general are less exposed to distorted information about the matter helps to
make the evolution more normal. When, however,
something occurs to thwart her progress, and an autoerotic type of activity threatens to gain permanent supremacy, then, whether the activity is conscious or not,
and whether distorted information comes to her ears or
not, a state of conflict usually rises. This state of conflict is certainly increased by misinformation from the
outside.

The neighborhood gang can be an important source
of valuable information, as well as trouble, for adolescent girls. In preadolescence the sexes tend for a time to
segregate. The girl as well as the boy seeks a "chum" of
her own sex. Girls also tend to congregate in gangs. It is
probable that in general these gangs are more loosely
organized than with the young male, although with the
development of organized athletics for girls and with
summer camps the situation tends to approximate that
of the boy. Neighborhood gangs under no adult direction and spontaneously created may have considerable
organization. The girl who is left out suffers the same as
the boy with a similar fate. The gang growing originally
out of girls who play together comes in time, especially
if the element of sex creeps in, to have as one of its

most important attributes that of secrecy. It is not always necessary to have an *important* secret but it is necessary to have an air of secrecy. There may be only a secret meeting place or there may also be a secret alphabet by which the members write notes to each other. The point is that the organization has secrecy, dignity, and contrives to keep the outsider outside.

Athletic interests are not, ordinarily, an important part of the girl gang. In the present-day gang they may be more important and perhaps were always so in certain groups. This is partly due to the passing of physical prowess with the beginning of the feminine life. The average girl must see boys who were her companions and rivals yesterday—boys whom in the past she could occasionally conquer—now, in fair fight, hopelessly outstrip her. The normal girl naturally does not long keep up her interest in an activity where she must soon be so obviously inferior.

* * *

Interest in sex plays an important part in the life of preadolescent groups of girls. They are profoundly interested in the physical changes they are undergoing. All bits of knowledge acquired from any source are talked over. There is some interest in the function of the males and the sexual act, but chiefly in relation to what are probably the most absorbing problems to girls' groups—pregnancy, masturbation, and menstruation. These topics have some of the fascination of danger. The distorted and terrifying data which girls with unreliable sources of information can acquire are remarkable. In general, girls who are members of gangs or similar groups are less likely to suffer from such serious misinformation. In the group there is a sifting of evidence, so to speak, and very often one member at least is well informed.

The fact that conflict about masturbation exists, without misinformation from the outside, makes it clearer in the case of the girl than in that of the boy that such conflict or panic arises not primarily from masturbation itself, but from the things it symbolizes in the personality, namely, the fear of isolation and the fear of failure to make the interpersonal adjustment.

In mid-adolescence problems of heterosexual relationships become more clearly apparent. In the first place, the attitude of the girl's immediate environment, especially that of the parents, changes toward her. Too often these parents begin to present added complications. The mother who has neglected her daughter's sexual education feels it incumbent upon her to do something about it at this stage. The things which are done in the name of safeguarding the girl's future happiness are to a great extent dependent upon the degree of normality in the mother's own love life.

The overanxious, suspicious mother constitutes a fairly frequent problem. Such a woman's attitude toward adolescence very briefly expressed is something like this: All boys are creatures possessed of dangerous animal instincts. All girls are their natural victims and must be protected from them. Her daughter is innocent and must therefore be carefully safeguarded. The mother is usually not frank with the girl chiefly because she has a personal repugnance to discussing the matter. She tends to control the situation by spying and prohibition. So the girl who may have led a life of comparative freedom up to adolescence suddenly finds her goings and comings matters of close supervision. The mother may talk to her vaguely about "bad boys," about the general lack of self-control of the male, or the daughter may be given lofty sentiments about her duty in uplifting boys and keeping them moral. At any rate, the upshot of the matter is that one must not be touched by a boy, and a kiss is a very serious matter. A girl may even worry over being ruined, being "damaged goods," if such a liberty is permitted. Girls who prior to adolescence have already fallen unduly under the sway of such a mother early become discouraged in their tentative efforts toward normal development. They cannot go out with boys without transgressing their standards— it therefore becomes easier to keep away from boys and to take refuge in the preadolescent relationship with girl friends.

An extreme example of a mother of this type just described is one who is frankly suspicious of the intentions of any boy paying any attention to her daughter. She may by her direct and indirect hints and questions succeed in making sex an ever-present preoccupation to the girl, so that she comes to feel it is the only reason for any social contact with the male. Then, she reacts according to her characteristic make-up, either by defiance, becoming promiscuous, or by complete retreat.

Another type of mother thwarts her daughter in a more insidious fashion. This is the mother who seeks to regain her own lost youth in her child's. In the cases which have come under my observation, the mother has always been a woman with strong unrecognized homosexual trends, who married for the sake of the prestige of marriage, who was not only frigid with her husband but also despised him. These women, as soon as adolescence approaches in their daughters, begin to participate actively in their daughters' little affairs. It is absolutely essential to them that their daughters be very popular—the number of boys calling on their girls is a matter of personal pride. They worm out of the girls the most detailed descriptions of their evenings, and on the basis of their greater experience they practically dictate the girls' thoughts and behavior. On the surface, such a mother seems to be aiding her child in development, but the real motivation of the attitude becomes apparent when the girl begins to show some real fondness for one boy. Then the mother's jealousy becomes active and she contrives in some way or other to break up the affair. This is often done by the most subtle criticism or ridicule of the boy, which finally leads the girl to feel that her judgment was very bad indeed to think there was anything desirable in the boy. A girl so dominated is entirely unable to make her own free choice. Her husband must be one of whom her mother approves, or none at all. She usually does marry because her mother would feel disgraced to have a daugh-

ter who did not, but her mother chooses the husband
and chooses a man whom the girl does not love, often a
man with definite homosexual leanings, in order to keep
the daughter's love for herself.

Another thing may be done by the mother who
relives her own adolescence in her daughter. She may
become personally interested in her daughter's friends,
cultivate their interest in herself, and win them away
from the daughter. Thus she strives to overcome her
jealousy of her daughter's youthful charm by the use of
her more sophisticated ways. The girl, too often, instead
of being angry with the mother and breaking from her
domination, has her feelings of inferiority increased and
receives a serious blow to her self-esteem.

But not only mothers create problems. The father
also has his share in complicating the life of his adolescent daughter. When the early father-daughter attachment has not been successfully resolved before adolescence, the father remains a person of great importance
in the emotional life of the girl. This is especially true if
there is some dissatisfaction in his own love life to turn
his interest to his developing daughter. His importance
may be so great that she does not become interested in
any other men. Sometimes she makes no attempt at all
to break away from the father—preferring his "pure
love" and protective care to the dangers of life. When
she does make the attempt, the father's reaction of
jealousy may reveal his feelings very clearly. The jealousy may be quite open but is often disguised; he may
wish to shield her from unprincipled boys, objecting to
this one or that one on some trivial grounds, and choosing one for her himself—a trustworthy boy (often homosexual)! Or he may not trust her with any male
escort, openly entering into competition himself—
taking her to parties and dances and watching carefully
the behavior of all of her partners.

*   *   *

Happy indeed is the girl who has parents who are
willing, when adolescence comes, to let the being they

have created and molded stand alone. The girl even more than the boy suffers from overprotection and overguidance, due almost entirely to the parents' problems and not the child's.

Even when the parents are not too involved in the situation and when the daughter has no clearly evident signs of earlier warping of her personality, serious traumatic experiences can come to a girl in adolescence.

Inexperienced gropings toward adulthood much more often meet with catastrophe for the girl than for the boy. It so happens that in our social order all premarital sexual activity for girls is strongly taboo. This is still true in spite of the development of a certain amount of tolerance in the last fifteen years in some groups. The penalty for transgression of this taboo when discovered is relatively great, amounting practically to social and economic ostracism. To be sure, a definite number of girls (psychopaths) violate this taboo deliberately. A smaller number, usually after the teens, violate the taboo deliberately and with understanding. We shall consider those later. At present, we are considering the sensitive, highly "moral" average girl who, by accident or inexperience, chiefly because she was not sufficiently aware of the driving power of her curiosity and emotions, is swept into such a situation, in itself not traumatic, but becoming traumatic because it violates her own standards. She is crushed by the thought of social disapproval. Should the situation through ignorance or accident result in pregnancy, the blow is very serious indeed. She seldom meets with any understanding at home, society has very little kindness for her, and she is confronted with the choice of illegitimate pregnancy, a premature and often unsuitable marriage, which does not make for the future happiness of anybody, or abortion. Any one of the three constitutes a serious blow to the developing personality.

Premarital sexual experience naturally does not affect all girls in the same way. Should it have been a love experience on the part of both participants, the end result may be something on the whole beneficial to the developing personality, rather than otherwise. Where the training has been very rigid, however, this is not true. The social taboo is so strong and parental training so rigid that seldom can a girl be found who can carry on a premarital affair without great anxiety and conflict.

In the casual premarital sexual experience, the girl usually suffers much more than the boy. Because she tends to have more conflict she takes the matter more seriously and more often expects to find love. She is then bitterly hurt and disillusioned when she finds she was but a passing fancy. Seduction of young girls by older men is often disastrous, because of the transient attitude of the man; and also in many instances because the girl had identified him with her father, or the father idea, and expected kindness and protection from him. However, in spite of the taboo and the suffering which may come to a girl from her experimentation with life, serious mental disorder results comparatively rarely from such a tragedy. The disasters resulting from masturbation conflicts, homosexual experiences, and unsuccessful and incomplete affairs with boys (such as relationships the importance of which are exaggerated in fantasy and later meet with rebuff from the boy) are more often precipitating factors of a schizophrenic illness.

Daydreaming, the great comfort of the isolated, often causes great concern among parents of adolescents. However, it may be an entirely healthy and creative activity, preparing for a fuller and more effective participation in reality. Daydreaming is closely connected with masturbation, but may exist without any physical manipulation. In general, the daydreams of adolescent girls are more predominantly erotic than those of the adolescent boy. The fact that girls are much less frequently given an opportunity for sublimation in the form of a career is probably to a great extent responsible for this. With the average girl—even when training for earning a living is acquired—it seldom has a life-long significance to her. Either consciously or half-consciously, she has in her mind the idea that she will do this—stenography or what-not—until she gets married. Sexual matters therefore have great importance in her life and usually take precedence in her daydreams and ambitions; for in the more normal, ambitions grow out of constructive fantasy. With the girl whose actual activities are not too much restricted, or whose personality has not already received too serious rebuffs, daydreams and actual experience are closely associated. She has fantasies about her popularity with boys and proceeds to make these fantasies come true in reality.

When the daydreams tend to replace reality, however, the situation is more serious. When overcoming parental resistance is too difficult, the girl tends to fall back on a dream life. When a father fixation or a mother fixation already exists, fantasy life tends to supplant reality. We then have an important factor for the development of serious disorder, and the mental disorder of prime importance in adolescence is schizophrenia. Pathologic daydreaming in girls rather typically proceeds somewhat as follows. A man who in some respects fulfills the girl's ideal for a mate enters her environment. We assume that the pathologic daydreamer already fears herself to be unsuccessful in the realm of reality. This man, however, may be friendly to her in a quite casual way, or he may be quite indifferent. He becomes the focus for her fantasy life. His activities are of great interest to her and she cultivates the acquaintance of all people who can give her information about him. Any chance remark of his is carefully treasured and studied so that she may understand any possible significance of it. In her fantasy, she is loved by him, she sees herself married to him—the envy of all her friends. If masturbation has been a problem, she suffers from her sexual excitement and struggles unsuccessfully with the old conflict. If masturbation has been more deeply repressed, she suffers from sleepless nights and restlessness.

In the meantime in the realm of reality nothing is occurring between her and the young man. The man is often entirely unaware of her interest, or he may be puzzled by her shyness or apparent self-consciousness in his presence. Should he by chance make any actual overtures toward her, the typical reaction on her part is flight. She contrives to drive him away in some fashion. But, if he continues indifferent or inactive, the fantasy goes on until tensions accumulate to the point where something must happen. The more normal of the day-dreamers then give up the interest or pass to a new one, deceiving themselves by some kind of rationalization for their failure. The more abnormal under this stress of emotion begin to lose the reality sense, and to believe in their own fantasy, until acting upon the fantasy some day they make some overt move, as, for instance, declaring their love to the man. They then usually meet with rebuff. The man is surprised and uncomfortable, and reacts accordingly. The girl may be plunged into illness—or into reality, depending on the severity of the blow to her. If the girl reacts with illness or, if this move to reality is omitted altogether, the girl begins to act as if she believed herself loved or married. We are then well into mental illness and fantasies substituted for reality, the end result being schizophrenia. The man does not necessarily have to be one personally known to the girl. An actor may be chosen or someone in that general position. A case occurs to me where the girl chose one of the violinists in an orchestra in a moving picture theater. She would go regularly to the theater and sit near the front, hoping that by chance he would look in her direction. If he did she would be happy for days, constructing her fantasies around the episode. It is possible if this type of dream life is not put to the test of reality that a girl may go on for years without a serious break. The case just described reached the age of twenty-nine before definite mental illness developed. What events in reality can occur to precipitate a schizo-phrenic illness in a girl? The above description of path-ologic daydreaming gives a clue to the onset in many cases. The rebuff from the man who has been chosen in fantasy may constitute a serious trauma. However, this trauma is not really in the realm of the love life—it has more to do with prestige and social success. To the woman, more than the man in our culture, marriage is an important goal for the establishment of prestige. It is still in most groups the only generally recognized mark of sexual success for a woman. When no real drive toward a heteroerotic love object exists, therefore, there may occur an artificial forced search for a mate with an exaggeration of her interest in the matter. The above-described fantasy love affair may be one result.

Another type of girl is able to be fairly successful with a man culturally or intellectually her inferior. Friendship with such a man furnishes the necessary social status for which she strives, namely, she can be seen with a man but she is ashamed of her man and suffers accordingly. She is also bored with him and gets no real pleasure out of his company. If her drive to do the socially successful thing succeeds in making her marry him, her mental illness is likely to develop later. Often, however, she passes from inferior man to inferior man, wondering why she never attracts men she can admire, heaping up inferiority feelings on that score, frequently developing a late schizophrenia. Sometimes a love relation with a man fifteen or twenty years the girl's senior, where the attitude of the man is primarily that of a father, is successfully achieved by a schizoid personality, and such a relationship may prove a stabilizing factor for years. But for these individuals a sexual partnership with an equal is impossible, because of the unconscious barriers constructed. In them the conscious wishes for sexual success are negated by the unconscious drives; the end result, in the total behavior, is that the man is antagonized or discouraged. At any rate, he is driven away. And the girl is usually entirely unaware of how she did it.

So much for the outward picture of preschizophrenia. What are the important precipitating factors in its actual development, given a girl who takes refuge in fantasy love affairs and avoids actual contacts with suitable men? What circumstances can bring about the panic state so often the beginning of a schizophrenic episode? It has been suggested that a crude rebuff from the man who has been the fantasy object may be the starting point. Back of this usually is panic over masturbation. The girl seldom brings herself to any overt move toward the man until sexual feelings have driven her to a point of desperation over masturbation. This panic may receive its precipitating stimulus from the outside or from within. A lecture on the evils of masturbation, or information from a book or friend on the question would be examples of precipitating stimulus from the outside. Usually there is some slight stimulus of this kind. Situations may occur, however, where it is not readily apparent why panic occurred at just that moment. In these cases, the frequent situation is this: The individual has strong resistance to masturbation, perhaps from earlier punishments temporarily forgotten. The fantasy life has gone on without manual manipulation, or some indefinite rubbing of the genitals has occurred. One day there is orgasm, and the result is panic. The feeling seems to be that something beyond her control has occurred; after it she felt confused or weak and thought she was losing her mind.

Another important factor in schizophrenic illness is homoerotic interest, especially if this is not fully conscious or is entirely unconscious. Given the daydreamer already described—carrying on a fantasy love affair with a man with whom she is slightly acquainted—it often occurs that this girl has an intimate friend to whom she confides selected bits of her fantasy, dressing them up as if they were reality. It is apparent that in the course of time the real love interest will be the girl confidante. Now should this girl confidante prove to be of a type tending toward overt homoerotic activity, a situation may arise for the daydreamer that will produce panic. It is characteristic of the preschizophrenic that all true object relationships are impossible. Any love relation with an approximate equal constitutes too grave a menace to the personality. This is especially true if the sexual element is introduced. A homoerotic love situation seems an even more serious menace than a heteroerotic one. This is possibly because the individual actually has greater capacity for homoerotic love and also because it steals on her unawares—a homosexual love situation not being part of her conscious ambition.

The question next arises what is likely to be the fundamental problem of the girl with tendencies to schizophrenia. Not sufficient work has been done on the matter yet to justify a definite statement. Certainly in the schizophrenic incest fantasies and delusions are very common. The belief that she is pregnant by her father is very frequent. One is surely justified in thinking there is a very strong father fixation. The deep psychoanalysis of one schizophrenic woman has led me to at least consider as a possibility an even earlier type of problem. The case mentioned showed on lay analysis that the important fixation in this girl was an attachment to the mother of the very early infantile type, namely, a fixation at the oral stage of libido development described by the psychoanalysts. Put in more popular terms, she was still seeking a love object toward whom she could have the complete dependency love of a nursing babe. It is possible that more data about schizophrenic women will confirm this. If so, it will show that schizophrenic women as well as men suffer from the nonresolution of the earliest type of infantile attachment to the mother.

The attitude toward homoerotic relationships in the girl differs from that in the boy in the same general way as the attitude toward masturbation. That is, there is much less general sentiment against it. Many people believe that homosexual experiences are limited to the male. Although the existence of "crushes" among girls is pretty generally recognized, their sexual significance may be denied. It is, in fact, sometimes denied by the individuals participating in the "crushes." Certainly an erotically tinged friendship in which embraces and kisses occur with frequency encounters very little social disapproval, and in fact it may be considered an accepted part of our culture. To this extent there is no taboo.

At the other extreme of the picture occurs the patterned homosexual—women with many "masculine" traits who have adopted the homoerotic way of life as a workable adjustment. These women on the whole perhaps make a better adaptation to life than men in a similar situation. They are fairly frequently women with successful careers. In general, they suffer less from the disapproval of society than a man in a similar position.

Of the in-between group of homoerotic women, there are a great number whose life history includes an occasional overt episode about which there is conscious or unconscious conflict and a great number who never progress beyond an intense "crush" stage. There are also the promiscuous homosexual "butch"-type women who affect masculine dress and mannerisms with the conscious intent of seducing women. These women are analogous to the homosexual "butches" in the male and should not be confused with a group of women who affect masculine ways and dress because they are not yet sufficiently aware of their difficulties. These latter women often are alarmed to find that they have the "same feelings for women," or at least for one woman in their group, and they hasten to cite their powers of attraction to men as proofs that they are not homosexual. They will sometimes say that they are just "so oversexed" that even women excite them. The real situation, however, seems to be that their promiscuous interest in men is an attempt to escape the homoerotic interest. These women, when isolated in groups of women, as in boarding schools or women's colleges, are very disrupting emotionally to those who come in contact with them. Because of their inability to restrain their impulses, their careers usually become definitely homosexual and they bring conflict and distress to many latent homosexuals. They then become the promiscuous homosexuals already described. Not all women who are promiscuous with men engage in overt homosexual activities by any means, for the homosexual factor underlying the promiscuity is very often unconscious, or at most but dimly recognized and evaded; and it is not the only motive in promiscuity. Hatred of men and revenge against some love object, recent or remote, are also factors.

Another type of woman who fails to make the heteroerotic goal, while apparently making it, is the girl whose self-love finds expression in a great need for popularity with boys. Many girls pass through this stage, and it is typically the last expression of the gang age. Some women never grow beyond it. With them to be adored by several men at once is a necessity. These women give very little affection, but are insatiable in their material and emotional demands on men. If their training has so constituted them that they must be true to husbands it is very difficult for them to make a choice for marriage. They are always tormented by the possibility of meeting a more interesting man later. After marriage, they are always discontented unless their moral code permits them some freedom. They must have adoration, platonic or otherwise. Homoerotic factors contribute to such a personality drive in the sense of gaining prestige and power with other women, but the narcissistic factor is probably more important. If their self-importance is not constantly fed they suffer from anxiety. Invalidism is one of the symptom formations which these women use when confronted with the passing of their sexual charm.

There remain to be discussed two other types of women who do not achieve heteroerotic adjustment. In referring to types it is not my intention to definitely define a group. It is merely used as a convenient method of description. Individuals often are combinations of more than one type. For example, it is apparent that the two types just described—the promiscuous woman and the woman whose main drive is for popularity— may occur in one individual, that is, promiscuity may be used in the service of popularity.

Rather characteristic of the female is the woman who makes her adjustment on the level of the preadolescent gang life with its patterned homosexual and autoerotic activity—typically the "crush" type. Such individuals occur in the male but, I judge, much more rarely. The female of this kind, on reaching adolescence, displays an almost total inability to accept any sexual adjustment as a legitimate part of her personality. She has a disgust reaction to sex, especially heteroerotic sex. She is uncomfortable with boys, but instead of retreating ex-

clusively into fantasy she clings to the safe uncompli-
cated life of preadolescence, and by denying (as far as
activity is concerned) the existence of boys, she man-
ages to "float" for many years without serious break.
Such women are prone to seek professions in which
they are thrown almost exclusively with women.
Among schoolteachers and Y.W.C.A. secretaries there
are a large number. Nevertheless, in spite of the sexual
revulsion, some women of this type marry. Social or
economic pressures and the desire for security are factors which force such women into marriage. The sexual
revulsion is never overcome. Sexual relations are endured as a wifely duty. Such women are not only frigid
but have no conscious regrets about their frigidity. On
the contrary, they are proud of their "purity." Whether
married or single, the characteristic object relationship
of this group is a rather etherealized friendship with
another woman or with several women. It is often a
mother-child relationship, especially when there is
marked difference in age. These women behave in their
conscious lives as if sexual impulses did not exist.
However, the impulses at times trick them into sexual
behavior; many struggle for years with masturbation—
never accepting it and feeling great guilt over it. Sporad-
ic homosexual episodes also occur, always with the
same type of conflict. The characteristic of this group is
the necessity to keep up the pretense that sex is not an
important part of life. These women often manage very
well with their adolescent type of interest until the
involutional period, when the fact that life is about to
pass them by is suddenly forced upon them. Then their
agitation and despair, coupled with violent self-
reproaches for what sexual activity has occurred in
their lives in spite of themselves, forms the characteristic picture of the involutional psychoses. Paranoid states
also may develop in this group. In general, it is a rather
nonaggressive type of paranoia characterized by a depressed, suspicious attitude toward the world, a state of
mind not necessarily incompatible with life outside an
institution. Obsessional personalities may also be found
in this group—"purity" in matters of sexual interest

being rather characteristic of the obsessional. These women very frequently have never been able to get away from home ties. In this group is the woman who "gives up" her life to her mother and who sometimes rationalizes her failure to marry as unwillingness to leave her mother alone. An early childhood tie to the parent has never been outgrown.

Another type of woman who does not reach true heteroerotic adulthood is the "modern" woman—the woman with a career whose ambition is to be a man among men. Our modern life is undoubtedly giving this woman an opportunity and making her life more tolerable. In fact, the relative ease of "careers" for women in modern life doubtless encourages some borderline women with feeble tendencies in this direction to enter the race. But the woman with the great inner drive to be a man has always existed. The most outstanding trait of such a woman is the necessity to be recognized as the equal of a man with the rights of a man. They seek in general the more definitely masculine professions—medicine, law, and business. They often seem to court struggle with prejudice, getting inordinate satisfaction out of victories against men. The really intelligent among them achieve a place in the masculine world and in time the respect of their male colleagues. The majority of them, however, become lost in the struggle and as the years go by develop an acid bitterness toward the male, blaming all failure to achieve the success they hoped for on the fact that they are discriminated against as women.

* * *

Such a woman sometimes marries, and the situation may be worked out if the husband has an appreciation of the difficulty and satisfactory concessions are made to her career. A few establish for themselves a free sexual life outside of marriage with lovers. A few become patterned homosexuals and, taking another woman as a wife, form a home. Such a situation sometimes works out well. But a great many find no stable sexual pattern. They may become very isolated individuals—they may engage in hectic flight from homosexual attachments, falling in the promiscuous group described. I suppose unhappy marriages to inferior men, or always living on the verge of a homosexual affair, comprises the form of maladjustment of the majority. In general, the woman with average training and ability desiring to be independent like a man is not happy. If nothing worse happens, she develops a chronic chip on her shoulder against the male. A paranoid development would be the typical psychotic result. These are the aggressive paranoids, the milder forms of which comprise the social or religious fanatic reformer. They may even become fanatic freethinkers preaching the gospel of "free love." Because of the relatively tolerant attitude of modern society, many of this group escape the clutches of mental disorder. Shall we say, they suffer from a socially successful maladjustment—that is, they lead useful and effective lives although with greater personal stresses and strains than others who come nearer to the norm?

"Penis Envy"

"Penis envy" is a term coined by Freud and used by him to describe a basic attitude found in neurotic women. The term had more than symbolic meaning to him. He was convinced that this envy in women grew out of a feeling of biologic lack beginning with the little girl's discovery in early childhood that she lacked something possessed by the little boy. Because of this, according to Freud, she believed she had been castrated, and she dealt with this shock either by sublimating the wish for a penis in the wish for a child, that is, becoming a normal woman, or by the development of neurosis, or by a character change described as the masculinity complex, a type of character which seeks to deny that any lack exists.

Critical evaluations of Freud's theory on the subject have already been published by Horney* and myself.† In brief, it has been shown that cultural factors can explain the tendency of women to feel inferior about their sex and their consequent tendency to envy men; that this state of affairs may well lead women to blame

---

* Karen Horney, *New Ways in Psychoanalysis* (New York: W. W. Norton, 1939), Chapter 6.
† Clara Thompson, "The Role of Women in This Culture," *Psychiatry*, IV (1941), 1–8; "Cultural Pressures in the Psychology of Women," *ibid.*, V (1942), 331–339.

all their difficulties on the fact of their sex. Thus they may use the position of cultural underprivilege as the rationalization of all feelings of inferiority.

The position of underprivilege might be symbolically expressed in the term penis envy using the penis as the symbol of the more privileged sex. Similarly, in a matriarchal culture one can imagine that the symbol for power might be the breast. The type of power would be somewhat different, the breast standing for life-giving capacity rather than force and energy. The essential significance in both cases would be the importance in the cultural setting of the possessor of the symbol.

Thus one can say the term penis envy is a symbolic representation of the attitude of women in this culture, a picturesque way of referring to the type of warfare which so often goes on between men and women. The possibility of using the term in two ways, that is, as actually referring to a biologic lack, or as symbolically referring to a feeling of inferiority, has led to some confusion in psychoanalytic writing and thinking. It would make for greater clarity if the term were used only in representing Freud's concept. However, as psychoanalysis has developed, new meanings and different emphases often have become attached to an old term without any attempt at precise restatement. Consequently, the term penis envy is used by many without very exact definition. This may lead one to assume that Freud's concept is meant when the thinking is actually along cultural lines. It, therefore, seems worthwhile to clarify the present-day meaning of the term.

It seems clear that envy of the male exists in most women in this culture, that there is a warfare between the sexes. The question to be considered is whether this warfare is different in kind from other types of struggle which go on between humans and if it is not actually different, why is there such preoccupation with the difference in sex? I believe that the manifest hostility between men and women is not different in kind from any other struggle between combatants, one of whom has definite advantage in prestige and position. Two things have contributed to giving the fact of sexual difference a false importance. Penis envy and castration ideas are common in dreams, symptoms, and other manifestations of unconscious thinking. Body parts and functions are frequent symbols in archaic thought. These ideas then may be only the presentation of other problems in symbolic body terms. There is not necessarily any evidence that the body situation is the cause of the thing it symbolizes. Any threat to the personality may appear in a dream as a castration. Furthermore, there is always a temptation to use some obvious situation as a rationalization of a more obscure one. The penis envy concept offers women an explanation for their feelings of inadequacy by referring it to an evidently irremediable cause. In the same way, it offers the man a justification for his aggression against her.

Sexual difference is an obvious difference, and obvious differences are especially convenient marks of derogation in any competitive situation in which one group aims to get power over the other.

Discrimination because of color is a case in point. Here, a usually easily distinguishable difference is a sign which is taken as adequate justification for gross discrimination and underprivilege. A Negro should feel himself inferior because he has a black skin. Obviously, the black skin is important to the group in power because it is such an easily recognized characteristic with which to differentiate a large number of people from themselves. Everything is done to make it a symbol for all the inferiority feelings Negroes have. Few indeed of the governing class can be so fatuous as to believe that black skin implies an intrinsic inferiority. It is amazing, however, to discover how near to this superficiality many of their rationalizations actually come.

In the same way, the penis or lack of penis is another easily distinguishable mark of difference and is used in a similar manner. That is, the penis is the sign of the person in power in one particular competitive setup in this culture, that between man and woman. The attitude of the woman in this situation is not qualitatively different from that found in any minority group in a competitive culture. So, the attitude called penis envy is

similar to the attitude of any underprivileged group
toward those in power.

The clinical picture of penis envy is one in which the
woman is hostile. She believes the man wishes to dominate her or destroy her. She wishes to be in a position
to do similar things to him. In other words, the penis
symbolically is to her a sword for conquering and
destruction. She feels cheated that she has not a similar
sword for the same purpose. This attitude need not
have a specific relationship to the sexual life and genitals as such, but may be found as a part of a more
general attitude of envy and may only secondarily
affect the sexual life. In fact, it may be accompanied by
evidences of envy in other relationships. Other women
who in some way have more assets and opportunities
may also be objects of envy. One may thus find a
woman supposedly suffering from penis envy showing a
general tendency to envy anyone who has something
she does not have and which she desires.

Envy is a characteristic of a competitive culture. It
implies comparison to one's disadvantage. There are
three general directions in which character can develop
in an effort to cope with this feeling. One outstanding
type of character development in Western society is the
one in which the person tries to excel over others. One
does away with envy by achieving success. If one fails
in proving that one is as good or better than the envied
one, tendencies to revenge may develop. The person
seeks then to pull the superior one down and in some
way humiliate him. Or a person may withdraw from
competition, apparently have no ambition, and desire to
be inconspicuous. In such a situation, although there
may be a feeling of helplessness and increased dependency, there may also be a secret feeling of power from
being aloof to the struggle.

As has been said, the relationship between men and
women has special features not found in the relationship with one's own sex. These special features are of
two kinds. They have to do with the attitude of a minority group to a dominant group, and they have to do
with the fact that the most intimate type of interperson-

al situation, the sexual act, is an important part of and usually exclusively limited to the relationship between the two sexes. Thus any problem of interpersonal intimacy would be accentuated in this relationship.

In a patriarchal culture the restricted opportunities afforded woman, the limitations placed on her development and independence give a real basis for envy of the male quite apart from any neurotic trends. Moreover, in an industrial culture in which the traditional family is no longer of central importance, the specific biologic female contribution, the bearing of children, loses value coordinate with the various factors which encourage a diminishing birth rate. This, although it is not a biologic inferiority, acts as if it were in that a woman can feel that what she has specifically to contribute is not needed or desired.

Therefore, two situations in the culture are of importance in this discussion: the general tendency to be competitive which stimulates envy; and the tendency to place an inferior evaluation on women. No one altogether misses some indoctrination with these two trends. If the competitive attitude is greatly developed by personal life experiences, the hatred of being a woman is correspondingly increased. The reverse is also true; that is, if there has been emphasis on the disadvantages of being a woman, a competitive attitude toward men tends to develop. Out of either situation may appear character developments which fit into the clinical picture of penis envy, and it is not necessary to postulate that in each case an early childhood traumatic comparison of genital organs took place. Such early experiences do sometimes occur, but it is my impression, as well as that of Fromm-Reichmann,* that they are traumatic only in the setting of other serious traumatic factors and that they derive their importance chiefly from offering a kind of rationalization for the feeling of inferiority and defeat.

One scarcely can overemphasize the fact that the

---

* Frieda Fromm-Reichmann, "Notes on the Mother Role in the Family Group," *Bulletin of the Menninger Clinic*, IV (1940), 132–148.

sexual relationship is one of the most important interpersonal situations. Any competitiveness in the personality of either participant is bound to have an effect
upon the sexual relationship. Any actual social underprivilege of one partner must also have an effect on the
sexual relationship. This should not be confused with
any idea that a biologic sexual inequality was the cause
of the competitive attitude or the condition of underprivilege of one partner. The sexual life is merely one
important situation in which the problem appears.

Thus it may be seen that the clinical picture of penis
envy has little to do with the sexual life, except secondarily, and that it has to do with all aspects of living. If
one rejects the idea that inferiority feelings in women
are due to a feeling of biologic lack, one must conclude
that the term does not describe a clinical entity deriving
from a constant origin, but has become a symbol and
rationalization for various feelings of inadequacy in
women. The situation of cultural underprivilege gives
the impression of validity to the rationalization.

Relations with Her Own Sex

All human beings, unless they are living under very unusual circumstances indeed, have some type of relationship with their own sex as well as with the opposite sex. This is not remarkable since about 50 per cent of the human race is of the same sex as oneself.

It is also not strange that the rules society makes about the way one should behave toward one's own sex are different from the rules of behavior toward the opposite sex. As is well known from the study of comparative cultures, customs concerning these relationships vary greatly from culture to culture. In ancient Greece, for example, a homosexual phase of development in the male was recognized and sanctioned. In Western culture today such an aspect of male relationship is not sanctioned. It is true that homosexual activity in early adolescence is recognized by the psychologically more sophisticated as a normal transient phase of development. But with this possible exception, all other homosexual activity in our society is not only considered abnormal, but also marks the unfortunate individual with a social stigma. In fact, according to the laws of some states, such a person is considered a criminal.

Because of this it seems unfortunate that, in developing his theory of bisexuality, Freud chose to use the word homosexual to characterize relationships with one's own sex whenever there was any degree of friendship or intimacy. The use of this term, with its derogatory implication, has, I believe, served to increase self-consciousness about friendly relations with one's own sex. For example, in Freud's partial analysis of an adolescent girl who had a crush on an older woman, the patient is labeled "homosexual" although no overt genital activity occurred.

The term has an even more damaging effect when it is applied to what is called unconscious homosexuality and latent homosexuality. It is my feeling that the use of such a term not only unnecessarily frightens the patient if the therapist uses it, but also tends to prejudice the therapist against the patient. Therefore, I have chosen to write about all types of intimacy between women, labeling only the situations with overt genital activity as homosexual.

Throughout childhood, there are no fixed rules about playmates. Boys and girls often play together before the age of eight. Sometimes groups of exclusively one sex or the other form. This banding together is reinforced by the unfriendly attitudes of the other group. In the case of girls, the boys of the neighborhood either try to ignore the girls altogether, or the relationship is one of teasing or bullying. This distinction between the sexes becomes more marked as preadolescence approaches.

However, if a girl happens to grow up in a neighborhood where most of her age group are boys, if she is a healthy child, she will find ways of making herself acceptable to them. She may, for instance, become a tomboy, that is, a baseball player, tree climber, or what-not. Similarly, a lone boy in a neighborhood of girls somehow gets himself included in the girls' games. His role is a little more difficult, because he is more likely to be teased about it at home. When and if he encounters boys of his own age group, they will be pretty rough about any "sissy" traits he may have acquired. But again, if he is a healthy boy, he will quickly outgrow any girlish characteristics he may have copied from his early playmates.

During the period of preadolescence, there is a greater tendency to segregation of the sexes. This is partly due to the inclination of young people themselves and partly to the influence of parental pressures. Often the mother says to her daughter, "You are getting too big to play with boys." What this means may be only vaguely apprehended by the girl. What she becomes increasingly aware of is that members of the opposite sex are different and that there are new rules connected with playing with them. Also, on a biologic level, there are stirrings which make association with the opposite sex in some way disturbing and exciting.

The parental attitude and the vague emotional discomfort combine to draw the sexes, for a time, toward their own kind. The chum appears. For the first time, the welfare and happiness of another human being becomes as important as one's own. The chum becomes the person to whom one tells one's troubles, ambitions, victories. She in turn reciprocates and together two kindred souls puzzle about the meaning of life.

Developing breasts and the appearance of pubic hair bring to the foreground, in the uninhibited, the exciting topic of sex. Rumors of menstruation and what it may mean are passed around. Children who have been fully informed become the teachers of others of their age. Or if there is no "wise" one among them, the uninitiated may resort to dictionaries, chance observations, or any other source of information available.

Boys of the same age are slower in becoming interested, but a little later they too pass through a similar period.

Both boys and girls have their secrets and the relationship with one's own sex is close. At first, there are small groups with a ganglike character. Then the groups tend to break up into twosomes, and there appears the best friend to whom one confides all. Mutual sexual feelings and experiences may or may not occur. But unless adults become concerned about it, there is no feeling of abnormality or guilt connected with the intimacy. This is the period of normal homosexual love.

As adolescence approaches, the healthy girl gradually turns her interest away from her chum toward boys. A frequent experience in this midway stage is the sharing of infatuation thoughts. Each remark, each overture of a boy is related in great detail to the girl friend. Together they speculate and giggle. In fact, part of the pleasure in attention from boys, at this time, is sharing the experience with the chum—until presently a special boy appears. Confiding in the chum becomes less important. Indeed, if one girl has reached the boy stage ahead of the other, her increasing indifference to the chum can cause many a reproach and heartache.

From adolescence until marriage, there is a growing absorption in the opposite sex. Double dating represents a remnant of the old chum relationship, but, on the whole, a girl's concern is with a boy—or boys.

It is very important to be popular, not only because it is fun in itself, but also because at this stage it increases one's value in the eyes of a particular boy. Still unsure of his own judgment, he is greatly reassured about the worth of the object of his interest if most of his fellow-companions are attracted to her, too. External appearance is very important at this stage. One must strive to be—as nearly as possible—the type in fashion at the time. This leads girls to become competitive with one another, and so it is a factor in breaking the chum relationship.

After marriage, most women in the United States turn again to their own sex for much of their companionship. During the long day, while the husband is at work, it is the woman friend with whom one shops, plays bridge, goes to the movies, gossips, and discusses things. Associating with other men in the absence of the husband is taboo in most American groups. Usually, a woman makes an appointment alone with a man other than her husband only if there is a business or professional reason for the contact. There are groups where this taboo no longer holds, but these are more emancipated groups, found chiefly in metropolitan areas.

Thus, relationship to one's own sex again becomes important. In fact, for the conventional woman, it becomes the only possible intimate relationship besides the one with her husband.

The degree of intimacy with other women, or another woman, may vary greatly, but, in some form, the greater proportion of a woman's waking life is spent with her own sex. Actually, in some communities, even evening social life shows a pretty complete cleavage of the sexes. At a dinner party only cocktails and the meal are shared. After dinner, the men play poker while the women gossip or play canasta—often in separate rooms. And even when there is no formal division, the conversations are likely to be separate: the men discuss business or politics; the women talk about children and domestics.

Thus the life of the middle-class American married woman is often almost entirely devoid of male companionship. Such isolation is not quite as true of her male partner, who at least has his secretary or women co-workers.

When the relationship between two women goes beyond mere social necessity and a degree of intimacy exists, we again find something comparable to adolescent discussion of boys. The topic this time is husbands, and perhaps sexual difficulties.

This, in brief, is the picture of the "normal homosexual" life of the American woman. If she has not been made self-conscious about her relation to women, she may spend many happy hours with her best friend—perhaps daily, while watching the children at play. There may be quite open demonstration of affection, such as hugging, walking arm in arm, even kissing. Women are still much freer in such matters than men, for whom the social taboo on demonstrativeness is stronger. On the other hand, especially in sophisticated groups, both men and women are becoming afraid to give any open demonstration of affection to a member of their own sex.

The borderline between a normal affectionate intimacy with a member of one's own sex and a pathologic homosexual attachment is not sharply defined. Thus, two adolescent girls (especially if they have been subjected to strict curtailment of contact with boys) may be inseparable, write love letters to one another, embrace, even fondle one another's genitals, without any permanent homosexual fixation. As soon as there is opportunity for association with boys, the intensity of their attachment to each other begins to diminish.

Later in life, similar situations are sometimes found. For example, a woman widowed in her fifties sometimes finds a younger woman to mother and love. With her, there may be, quite definitely, the feeling that caring for somebody—almost anybody—is better than no love at all. The younger woman in this situation may be more pathologically homosexual.

Or, two women in their fifties may become attached to each other. I once had such a case. My patient, a very dependent person, had for years been bitterly disappointed in her husband, who was unambitious and just barely managed to make a living. As a result of brief analytic work, she was able to turn her affections toward a woman who had many of the qualities her husband lacked. This woman was successful, a good companion, affectionate, and also had money to spend. The two spent many happy years together. In fact, their relationship continued until my patient's death.

Certainly, one cannot say there was no pathology here. A less dependent type would possibly have ended the unhappy marriage earlier and found a new heterosexual partner. However, there were cultural obstacles, as well as neurotic difficulties, in the way of this, for my patient lived in a small Western town where her generation, at least, frowned on divorce. It would have taken more courage than she had to make a definite break. And she would certainly have suffered some social ostracism if she had left her husband or taken a lover, whereas the appearance of a close woman friend made no particular difficulty for her.

On the other hand, a case which may look as if the homosexuality had developed chiefly because of a difficult situation may prove, on deeper probing, to be a true pathologic situation. For example, one woman who consulted me, concerned over her increasing homosexual cravings, had shown no particular interest in women prior to her marriage, or for several years thereafter. The homosexual longing seemed to erupt in response to sexual difficulties with her husband. During the third year of marriage, he developed premature ejaculation. As a result, the wife was frequently left in a state of unsatisfied sexual tension. She came to loathe the sight of her husband's erect penis, and a flood of homosexual fantasies began. She soon became infatuated with another woman who was somewhat (but not entirely) inclined to reject her advances.

On the surface, one might say, this woman did the best she could under the circumstances. Feeling completely frustrated in her relationship to a male, she turned to a woman for satisfaction.

However, the situation was not so simple. The husband's increasing sexual difficulty could be traced partly to the patient's attitude toward him. Her dissatisfaction with him as a person and as a sexual partner were being conveyed to him before the beginning of his sexual difficulty. This woman's deep longing was to be mothered. She wanted to be cared for and to have nothing expected of her in return. This longing was buried. Prior to her marriage, she was an intensely competitive person. She had to be the best in everything. She made a "good" marriage, socially speaking, and for a time she liked her husband because he was evidence of her success. But after the birth of her child (a girl), her repressed longing to be in the position of the baby began to force itself on her awareness. So, in spite of the superficial picture, her homosexuality turned out to be a pretty basic problem and not merely an expedient to help her over a difficult time in her marriage.

In studying the overt homosexual life of women, one is struck by certain differences from the problem of the male. In the first place, society looks on the homosexual woman with more tolerance than it does the homosexual man. Several factors contribute to this. Heterosexual experience potentially has more serious consequences for the female than the male. There is the ever-present possibility of pregnancy, which inevitably inhibits free experimentation with sex. Two homosexual women, both of whom were also married, told me that they felt that one reason why they found more satisfaction in their homosexual relations with each other than in relations with their husbands was because there was no need to consider contraception. This was undoubtedly a rationalization of their activity and should not be given too much weight, but it was nonetheless a small factor.

Moreover, the double standard of permissiveness for sexual behavior still has some social influence on society's attitude toward the heterosexual activities of the female. The disapproval of heterosexual incontinence is, in most communities, stronger than the disapproving attitude toward a woman's sexual attachment to one of her own sex. In fact, a Lesbian, who had been living quite openly with a woman for many years without feeling guilty, was shocked and disgusted when she learned that another woman friend of hers had a male lover. To her, sex with a man outside of marriage was immoral. She broke her friendly relations with this woman and felt very self-righteous about it.

Another woman, who was having difficulties in her marriage, was on one occasion attracted to another man and almost made up her mind to have an affair with him, but became very frightened at the prospect. The fear seemed to be largely due to her conventional training. At any rate, on the day she had decided to take the plunge, she met a woman who attracted her greatly. She dropped all thoughts of the man and immediately began to court the woman, telling herself, "Here is a nice safe solution." Of course, this is not the whole story, but in this case a strong conditioning against heterosexual freedom seems to have been an important factor in her homosexual interests.

Other factors, originally connected with the greater concern about the heterosexual activities of the female, also still hamper a woman in freely seeking the companionship of men. For instance, there is still some feeling that she should not be aggressive in seeking a man. Some of the popular comments about a woman who shows sexual eagerness express the general attitude of contempt for her behavior. One hears: "She acts like a bitch in heat," or "Is she trying to get her hooks into him?" and so forth. Whereas a man is permitted to be rather proud of being a "wolf." Therefore, in seeking a heterosexual partner, women still have to resort to in-direct methods—and this too makes it easier to seek a homosexual mate.

Also, women living alone in large cities have very few opportunities to meet men, except through their work. If, as in the case of teachers and social workers, they are in a predominantly female profession, they may literally have no means of contacting men without making very determined efforts in that direction. And, in accordance with convention, these efforts must also be discreetly indirect. Granted that many women with homosexual tendencies choose such professions, there are also many who become homosexual with but slight initial inclination in that direction.

Still another practical factor weighs the scales some-what in favor of a tolerant attitude toward homosexual-ity for women. The physically unattractive woman has more difficulty in finding a partner of the opposite sex than a physically unattractive male. In fact, the situa-tion is completely reversed. For the male, physical de-fect or aging make the homosexual way of life more hazardous, whereas beauty or youth in the male is not a prerequisite for success with women. In the case of women, the woman with some physical blemish may more easily find a woman than a man as a sexual partner. Hence, many women drift into a homosexual life because they have no confidence in their powers to attract men.

On a somewhat deeper level, another factor also seems to play a part in the greater tendency to accept female homosexuality. In many Lesbian couples, one of the pair affects masculine behavior and often man-nish attire. This does not attract the degree of ridicule which the assumption of feminine behavior in the male does.

Although an extremely mannish attitude may call forth some comment, the tailored woman, the girl who is good at sports and can take hard knocks "like a man," is beginning to become the American ideal; whereas even small traces of so-called feminine mannerisms, a little too precise concern for personal appearance in a man, are somewhat objectionable to most people.

This may stem from childhood attitudes, when the little boy who is afraid to play rough games and is kept wearing curls too long is jeered at as a sissy, but the tomboy, the girl who plays boys' games and will even fight a boy if he tries to bully her, is usually admired by her contemporaries, both male and female. So it would seem that both in childhood and in adult life, masculine traits are revered and feminine ones belittled; that, further, many less praiseworthy traits are dubbed feminine for no very adequate reason. In short, the fact that at present the tendency is to aspire to the male way of life makes the masculine woman more socially acceptable than the feminine man.

These various facts leave their imprint on the general attitude toward homosexuality in the male and female. Even more basic and in a sense truly biologic is another consideration making female homosexuality more acceptable than male. The most important early influence in everyone's life is the mothering one. With the female, this early tie is with a member of her own sex. The satisfaction of her earliest physiologic needs came from a woman. So, the female homosexual is returning to something which has been experienced in infancy, i.e., physical contact with a member of her own sex. The male homosexual may also be seeking a mother, but for some reason cannot endure physical contact with a woman and must find a mother in a man.

The question arises whether any one of these considerations may, in itself, be a cause for homosexuality in the female. Homosexuality in either sex (especially when it is the only form of sexual relationship) must, I think, be considered a part of a pathologic personality picture. The fact that there is greater social tolerance of the situation in regard to women does mean, however, that many women become homosexual who are suffering from relatively mild personality deviation. In general, homosexuality in the male is connected with more severe psychopathology.

I do not wish, however, to leave the impression that there are no very deeply disturbed female homosexuals. One encounters them, but the proportion of the total number is less.

Here I should like to mention a detail, the significance of which I am not prepared to estimate; but I believe it does have a significance. One frequent form of male homosexual activity is, according to my experience, seldom found in the female, and that is interest in anal stimulation. One can, of course, say there are practical reasons for this; since the woman has a vagina, she has no need for a vagina substitute, a role which the anus plays, to some extent, for the male. But anal activity also has other meanings in male experience. Because of its painful aspect, it is also an expression of sadomasochism; and because of society's attitude, it is also an expression of contempt. It is probably the most pathologic form of sexual activity, if we try to evaluate sexual activity as an expression of the level of personality integration. And its relative infrequency in women may be another indication that, in general, homosexual behavior is part of a less pathologic picture than is often the case with men.

Although the relatively tolerant attitude of society may make it easier for women to choose homosexuality as an expression of their neurotic difficulties, it is not the cause of homosexuality as a neurosis. For this, one must look to unsatisfactory early relationships. In psychoanalysis, there is always an attempt to uncover the background of a given personality development; in the life history of the homosexual woman, certain experiences and situations appear frequently. However, these situations do not always produce homosexual women, and therefore we cannot say that they are the specific cause. In fact, at the present time, one cannot say that there is a specific sequence of events which invariably makes a person a homosexual.

Constitutional predisposition was questioned early by Freud, and is even more searchingly questioned today. Even male castrates show no decided tendency to become homosexual. The basic body build does not seem to determine a tendency. There are about as many broad-hipped men, with a tendency to breast formation and feminine hair distribution, among heterosexuals as among homosexuals. Similarly, the narrow-hipped, breastless female just as often marries, has children, and proves to be as adequately maternal as does the more conventionally feminine woman.

When one comes to effeminate mannerisms in the male, and masculine or boyish mannerisms in the female, one is no longer dealing with constitution, but with personality development. In other words, these are expressions of acquired attitudes and are often, although not necessarily, connected with homosexual interest.

Seduction by a member of one's own sex in childhood or adolescence may be the final precipitating factor in determining the form a neurosis may take. Thus, a person with the possibility of homosexual development may become schizophrenic or obsessional or show some other character difficulty, if he does not happen to have been exposed to sexual experience with his own sex. On the other hand, as I have already suggested, overt homosexual experience cannot make a relatively healthy person homosexual. The situation is comparable to that of alcoholics. Many people drink in moderation and do not become alcoholic, while others avoid serious addiction only by staying away from alcohol altogether.

In the course of the analyses of homosexual women, one finds certain types of early experience frequent. One probably first thinks of the woman with a strong masculine identification. The desire to be a boy is usually found very early in such people. There is a revolt against being a woman and living the usual life of a woman.

In the latter part of the last century and the beginning of this one, women of this type were frequently found in the forefront of the struggle for emancipation of women. Many suffragettes and many pioneers in the professions were women who had definitely renounced home and marriage. They usually had a hatred and contempt for man at the same time that they strove to be like him. It is possible that the times—that is, the Victorian era with its strongly repressive influence on the expression of a woman's capabilities—acted as a goad in stimulating the rebellion of these women. But, wherever the need to act in a masculine way was deepseated in the personality, it is my experience that, in addition, specific early difficulties in the given person's life contributed definitely.

Frequent among these is the family's disappointment that the child was not a boy. This is early conveyed to the child in varying ways. There may be simply unspoken disappointment and regret which the child senses; or there may be open reference to it; or one parent or the other may try to make a boy of the child. For instance, the father tries to mold his daughter to an interest in the career he had hoped a son would seek. In these cases the type of man-to-man companionship the girl has with her father often influences her later relationship to men. She seeks to be one of the boys rather than to be a woman to them. This situation need not reach pathologic proportions if the girl's relationship in the family is otherwise good, that is, if she feels loved and accepted for herself also. In fact, there is much to be said for a woman who can be companion as well as lover to a man. It assumes the proportions of the masculinity complex only when the need to be one of the boys is the most important aspect of a girl's relationship to men.

Another situation which may produce lasting penis envy, that is, envy of the male and his privileges, is a home environment in which a brother is much preferred. The parents may be more indulgent to him, less strict in discipline, and, especially in families of limited income, readier to make sacrifices for his education or interests.

However, neither of the above life experiences needs to end in homosexuality. They merely constitute pushes in that direction.

When one analyzes these strikingly masculine women, one finds that the boyish swagger, the scorn for attractive clothes, is a defensive façade. Under it is a shy, withdrawn person, ill at ease and in need of mothering, although often unable to accept mothering. One such person stated that her mother had often told her that, even as a very small child, she could not tolerate being hugged. She would sit stiffly, bolt upright in the mother's lap, and squirm away as soon as possible. In later life, she showed the same uneasiness under any demonstration of affection. Her boyish manner represented a neurotic need for independence. She could accept loving attention only from someone who was dependent on her. This was the situation in her homosexual ménage. She was the man of the family, but she was also the little child.

Since the personality of the child is first influenced in its formation by interaction with the personality of the mother, an understanding of the emotional needs of the mother is important. In the above case, the mother proved to be a woman, herself very much in need of reassurance as to her worth. She was timid and anxious, but covered this with a stern stoicism, and a tendency to be derogatory of others. She unwittingly depended on the love of her child to satisfy her own needs. Her desire to pet the child was not affectionate tenderness, with concern for the child, but an evidence of her own love craving. Even the little child reacted to her advances as to a danger.

As the child grew older, the mother's disinterest in her welfare became more apparent. She made no effort to dress the girl attractively. (In fact, one neighbor was sufficiently concerned about the neglect of the child's personal hygiene to take a hand herself and once washed the girl's hair. This made the girl feel humiliated, although she was not old enough at the time to

have been expected to take the responsibility herself.)
As the girl entered adolescence, the mother—apparently
threatened by her daughter's budding attractiveness—
constantly made derogatory comments about her pos-
ture, her clothes, her hair-do, until the girl, already
sufficiently unsure of herself, gave up all interest in her
personal appearance and became more and more boyish in dress and manner. It is not strange that she fell in
love with the first woman who took an interest in her
and appreciated her. This love ended in disaster, because, after a few blissful months, the other woman
became moralistic about their sexual activity and in-
sisted on stopping the relationship. Again, a mother had
found the girl reprehensible! Only years later did she
learn that the actual reason for the change in attitude
was that the other woman had fallen in love with
someone else. This, in brief, is a characteristic history
of one type of homosexual woman.

Not all homosexual women have a marked masculinity complex. There is the maternal type, who often
seeks a younger woman and makes a home for her. At
first glance, one may think it is mere accident that such
a woman did not marry and rear a family. Indeed, in
the days when being married was a fairly essential
career for a woman, many of them did marry and were
also homosexual. Even here, the really important tie
was to the woman.

A study of these cases also reveals early pathology.
Unlike the boyish woman who struggled against the
mother's possessiveness, one case was a woman who did
not break the early ties with her mother, but remained
absorbed in and absorbed by the mother. In adult life,
she reversed the pattern, playing the mother's role.
Here the early family situation is also significant. The
mother was a frigid woman who endured sex only as a
duty. She early began to indoctrinate her daughter with
the horrors of childbirth. She painted a picture of a
woman's life as one of suffering without reward. In this
case, the father took no interest in his female child.
Frightened by the mother's story, unable to get the
attention of the father, this woman could not go

through the normal developmental experiences and came to adolescence without interest in the opposite sex.

A third type of early childhood history is also found in homosexual women. This is where the mother was unloving and self-centered, and there was seduction—or near seduction—of a more or less gratifying nature by the father. Here we have several factors, combining in adolescence, to keep the girl from turning toward men of her own age. She finds young men too inexperienced, and unable to give her the things she receives from the father. This weakens her own inner drive to seek a mate. At the same time, the father is jealous of any rival, and this also deters her. In addition, it has often been necessary to appease the mother, all through childhood, because of the father's preference for the daughter. This competition becomes increased in adolescence, so that, in an attempt to gain the favor of a mother who never paid much attention to her, the girl may turn from men altogether and leave the field free for the mother.

On the other hand, when seduction by the father is predominantly an act of lust, without affection, with or without subsequent guilt on his part, and he later turns away from the child in either indifference or shame, the man becomes, in the girl's eyes, a beast to be feared and avoided.

In short, the following situations, individually or in various combinations with one another, may predispose a girl to homosexuality: anything which develops the masculinity complex with its neurotic need for independence or control; any attitude of hatred or disgust for men on the part of the mother; too strong erotic interest in the girl on the part of the father; too great indifference or hostility in the father, which tends to make the girl cling to the mother; jealousy and competitiveness on the part of the mother, which causes the girl to withdraw from the heterosexual field.

These examples probably do not exhaust the possible early influences and do not specifically determine the choice of an overt homosexual life. They do undoubtedly produce serious personality disorder, and homosexuality is one of the possible attempts at a solution.

There are about as many different types of homosexual relationships among women as there are among men, but it is my impression—and Kinsey's report supports it—that relatively permanent relations, with genuine affection, are more frequent with women. These twosomes also come nearer to approximating a normal social relationship with others, and here the comparative absence of society's disapproval is a factor.

The promiscuous homosexual woman does exist; also the woman who does not remain interested in any one woman very long. On the other hand, I have not found among women anything comparable to the male who seeks fleeting genital contacts in public toilets and parks, although there are some who pick up other women at bars. But even here, there seems to be a little more to the relationship than mere genital interest.

One reason for this apparent difference between male and female homosexuals is undoubtedly cultural. Women's public toilets do not faciliate such encounters, whereas men's do. Also, there seems to be entirely lacking, in the female, a need to compare genitals, or to display genitals as such. The female sexual need seems to be rather to have the whole body admired, and this cannot be done easily in public places.

To summarize, the life of the average homosexual woman in our culture is more often carried on within the acceptable framework of our social customs than is that of the male homosexual. The latter tends more to form a subculture; that is, a social group with different values and customs, and even, to some extent, a different vocabulary from those of conventional society.

One must note that the more disturbed (or rebellious) types of homosexual women also tend to congregate in groups which pride themselves on being different from the rest of mankind, and these deviant groups often tend to associate themselves in friendly symbioses with the male homosexual society.

A discussion of woman's relation to her own sex

would be incomplete without mention of the women who have great difficulties in relating to their own sex. These women fall roughly into three categories.

There are women who experience great difficulty in all forms of intimacy. They are withdrawn, often schizoid, types who either remain fairly isolated, or have a great number of contacts, none of which has important emotional value. These are severely damaged people, for whom there has been no significant experience of tenderness in childhood.

The second type takes in those who see relationships to women largely in terms of competition for men. With these, feelings for other women are either indifferent or hostile and competitive. Such a woman never cultivates female friendships. Her sole interpersonal interest is a varying degree of pursuit of the male for security purposes. She may be engaged in an unconscious flight from homosexuality. Or she may be carrying on the endless battle with other women for possession of men; possibly a continuation of the early Oedipus struggle with the mother. Or all of her energies may be concentrated on some destructive attitude toward the male, characterized by her attempts to conquer and control him.

The third type of woman who cannot relate to women establishes a kind of symbiosis with homosexual men. She may have a very good friendly relationship with one or more homosexual men. She is accepted by them, and is sometimes used as a front to deceive the world. In other words, they date her, like to be seen in public with her, but nothing sexual happens between them. She is a part of their public social life; she may even know all about their affairs. But her own life is unfulfilled. She is treated like one of the boys, in one sense, and yet she is forever outside. Her relationship is with people who cannot possibly relate intimately to her because of their own problems.

Often such a woman has insufficient insight into her own role and may keep hoping that one or another of her companions will marry her. In fact, such a marriage does occasionally take place, but I believe it is, invariably, anything but a happy solution. I probably have no right to generalize from my few cases in this area, but it is my impression that many of these women think of themselves as men among men. In other words, this is an expression of the masculinity complex. They do not desire a sexual relationship with men, but for some reason they have not become homosexual.

Others in this group are women who cannot believe they can be accepted by either sex. By relating themselves to the type of male who must reject them, they perpetuate their own conviction. They have no friends of their own sex, and in the group of male homosexuals, they remain the outsider. In short, women who cannot have a good relationship with their own sex cannot have a satisfying relationship with men either. Capacity for genuine affection for members of one's own sex is essential for healthy human relationships in general.

Changing Concepts of
Homosexuality in Psychoanalysis

The term "homosexual" as used in psychoanalysis has come to be a kind of wastebasket into which are dumped all forms of relationships with one's own sex. The word may be applied to activities, attitudes, feelings, thoughts, or repression of any of these. In short, anything which pertains in any way to a relationship, hostile or friendly, to a member of one's own sex may be termed homosexual. Under these circumstances, what does an analyst convey to himself, his audience, or his patient when he says the patient has homosexual trends? It does not clarify much in his own thinking, nor convey a definite idea to his audience. When he uses the term in talking with the patient, his words—instead of being helpful—often produce terror, for in ordinary speech the word "homosexual" has a much more specific meaning, and in addition a disturbing emotional coloring.

In view of the general confusion, it has seemed to me worthwhile to review the whole subject, trace the various psychoanalytic ideas about homosexuality, and, finally, describe the status of the concept today.

Freud, in accordance with his libido orientation, considered unconscious homosexuality something basic and causal in neurosis, while more recent analysis has led to the conclusion that homosexuality is but a symptom of more general personality difficulties. Instead of being the basic problem in a given case, it is but one of the manifestations of a character problem and tends to disappear when the more general character disturbance is resolved. From Freud's point of view, unconscious homosexuality is to be found in everyone. It is a part of the original libido endowment. According to him, it may exist in three different forms. There is latent homosexuality, repressed homosexuality, and overt homosexuality. Latent homosexuality apparently exists in everyone, although perhaps the amount varies from one person to another. It is not necessarily pathological. Freud assumes it may either find expression in pathological difficulties or in sublimation. Psychoanalysis has to deal with homosexuality as a problem only in its repressed or overt forms. If the use of the term were limited to these two forms, there would be less confusion, although even here Freud speaks of repressed homosexual trends in situations where the sexual content in the usual limited sense of the term does not exist.

Freud's view of the matter is based on his concept of bisexuality. According to him a part of the original libido endowment is allocated to homosexuality. This libido apparently cannot be converted into heterosexual libido. The two remain distinct and are a part of the original bisexuality. In the course of development, one of the two wins out, and the loser either becomes sublimated or is the foundation for the formation of neurotic difficulties. So in Freud's theory unconscious homosexuality is an important ingredient of basic personality structure. It has never been clear to me under what conditions Freud thought these unconscious tendencies became conscious or overt.

The inverted Oedipus complex is presented as the starting point of homosexual development. In some situations also a regression to narcissism is thought to favor the development of homosexuality, since loving a member of one's own sex may be thought of as an extension of love of oneself. However, even if one accepts Freud's formulation, this description does not explain the dynamics of the process. It is still necessary to know what specific life experiences produced the inverted Oedipus or the regression to narcissism, and why regression to narcissism does not always produce overt homosexuality. Freud suggests that a possible determinant may be varying strengths of original homosexual endowment. Resort to constitution as an explanation very often simply means—the necessary information is not yet available.

One confusion in the literature arises from the fact that cases are sometimes reported as examples of homosexuality where no clear-cut sexual relation existed, but only a strong neurotic dependency on a member of one's own sex was demonstrated. One is left to assume that there is no difference in the dynamics of such a case and one with definite overt manifestations. As far as I know, there has been no analytic data in the classical school on what produces the final violation of cultural taboo when the person accepts an overt homosexual way of life, except the very general idea that such a person has a weak superego, that is, he is unable to control the direction of his libido drives.

If Freud's basic theory of personality is questioned, that is, that the character structure is the result of the sublimation of sexual drives, the problem of repressed and overt homosexuality has to be approached differently. When the libido formula is discarded, it is much easier to see that homosexuality is not a clinical entity. There is no clear-cut situation in which it invariably occurs. It appears as a symptom in people of diverse types of character structure. The simple division into active and passive types does not cover the picture, nor are these distinctions always clear-cut. For example, the same person may be active with a younger partner and passive with an older one. The personality type who happens to have made an overt homosexual adjustment in one case may be almost identical with the personality type who under very similar circumstances makes a heterosexual choice in another case. Robbins* describes the competitive and exploitative personalities as characteristic of homosexuals. However, as is well known, competitive and exploitative heterosexual situations are also very frequent. So the specific choice of the sex object is not explained in Robbins' paper.

One can agree with Freud that all people are not only bisexual but polysexual in the sense that they are biologically capable of being sexually roused by either sex, or in fact by a variety of other stimulants. Many people tend to form a more or less lasting attachment to the partner in their sexual pleasure. In childhood before the taboos of adults are imposed, a state of uncritical enjoyment of body stimulation exists. When the pleasure is shared, it may be shared with either sex depending to a great extent on propinquity or availability.

On the basis of the early childhood example, it would be interesting to speculate about what might happen if a person could continue his development in a culture with no sex restrictions. It is possible that most children would eventually develop a preference for the biologically most satisfactory type of sexual gratification and that that would prove to be found in the union of male and female genitals. If it should be found that heterosexual activity eventually became the preferred form of sex life, would this mean that the other forms had been repressed? If the culture were truly uncriticizing, repression would be unnecessary. Homosexuality would disappear when more satisfactory gratifications were available. It might reappear if the heterosexual possibilities were withdrawn. In other words, it is probable that on the physiological level uninhibited humans would get their sex gratification in any way possible— but if they had a choice, they would choose the most pleasurable. However, most sexual relationships, in addition to the physiological gratification of lust, have meaning also in interpersonal terms. The relationship as

* Bernard S. Robbins, "Psychological Implications of the Male Homosexual 'Marriage,'" *Psychoanalytic Review*, XXX (1943), 428–437.

a whole has significance. The value of the relationship in turn affects the satisfaction obtained from the sexual activity. Except in some situations, to be described presently, in which the choice of a homosexual love object is determined by environmental limitations, it would seem that the interpersonal factors—that is, the type of relationship, the nature of the dependency, the personality of the love object—cannot be overlooked in determining whether the choice is a heterosexual or a homosexual way of life. Before discussing this in detail, it would be well to look at some of the varying degrees of acceptability of homosexuality in our own society.

Some form of sexual restriction is found in most cultures. There is a preferred and acceptable form of sexual behavior while other forms of sexual gratification are in varying degrees of disrepute—some being absolutely forbidden and punishable, others simply less acceptable. It is obvious that, under these circumstances, no individual is free to choose. He has to cope with the danger of ostracism if he is driven toward a culturally unacceptable form of sexual behavior. This is definitely one of the problems associated with overt homosexuality in our culture, especially in the case of men.

Freud believed one important distinction between a repressed and an overt homosexual was that the former had a stern superego and the latter a weak superego. This is too simple a statement of the problem, for among overt homosexuals one finds, in addition to the psychopaths who answer to Freud's description, those people who suffer from superegos and are genuinely unhappy about their condition; others who accept their fate with resignation but feel handicapped; and still others who have lost all sense of self-esteem and think of their sexual behavior as but another evidence of their worthlessness. Also some more fortunate cases through protected circumstances have not happened to come in contact with the more criminal psychopathic elements in homosexual groups, especially in large cities, and because of their isolation or discreet living have not been made acutely aware of society's disapproval.

These homosexuals do not feel great conflict about their relationship, although in other respects they are not lacking in a sense of social responsibility, that is, they do not have weak superegos, to use Freud's term.

Women are most frequently found in the last-named situation. This brings us to a consideration of the difference between male and female homosexuality, at least in this culture. Women in general are permitted greater physical intimacy with each other without social disapproval than is the case with men. Kissing and hugging are acceptable forms of friendly expression between women. In America a father is often too self-conscious to kiss his own son, while mother and daughter have no such inhibitions. Ferenczi* pointed out that in our culture compulsive heterosexuality is one outgrowth of the taboo on even close friendship with one's own sex. It is obvious that in the case of women there is a much more permissive attitude about friendship with one's own sex and therefore about overt homosexuality. Until recent times there was a much stronger taboo on obvious nonmarital heterosexual situations. Two overt homosexual women may live together in complete intimacy in many communities without social disapproval if they do not flaunt their inversion by, for example, the assumption of masculine dress or mannerisms on the part of one. Sometimes even if they go to this extreme they are thought peculiar rather than taboo. On the other hand, two men attempting the same thing are likely to encounter marked hostility.

Perhaps this difference in the attitude of society has a deep biological origin, to wit: Two women may live together in closest intimacy with kisses, caresses, and close bodily contact without overt evidence of sexual gratification; two men in the same situation must know that they are sexually stimulated.

Whether this biological factor contributes to the increased tolerance for female homosexuals or not, there are other factors which definitely contribute to making

* Sándor Ferenczi, *Selected Papers,* ed., Ernest Jones (3 vols.; New York: Basic Books, 1950), Vol. I. *Sex in Psychoanalysis.* See Chapter 12, "The Nosology of Male Homosexuality."

the situation more normal in women. Earlier in the discussion I pointed out that in situations of limited choice a person makes the best of the sexual partner available. If there is a wide range of choice, a person chooses the most desirable. Circumstances producing privation—such as army life in remote places—may make strange creatures attractive as sex objects. However, in general men encounter fewer external causes of deprivation than women. So when a man becomes an overt homosexual it is almost always because of difficulties within himself. Of these society is not tolerant. It tends to label the man as weak. Women are more frequently in an isolated situation with regard to heterosexual possibilities than men. Age and physical unattractiveness handicap women more. More conventions surround her search for a partner so that even when young and attractive she may find herself for long periods without socially acceptable means of meeting men. Thus strong external difficulties often lead relatively mature women into homosexual relationships, whereas overt homosexuality in the male is usually an expression of grave personality disorder. I do not wish to imply that there are no severely disturbed homosexual women, but rather that society's tolerance may be traced to the greater proportion of fairly healthy homosexual women.

The different cultural attitudes toward the sissy and the tomboy again show society's greater tolerance for the female homosexual type. When a boy is called a sissy, he feels stigmatized, and the group considers that it has belittled him. No such disapproval goes with a girl's being called a tomboy. In fact she often feels considerable pride in the fact. Probably these names get their value from childhood ideas that courage and daring are desirable traits in both sexes. So the sissy is a coward, a mama's boy, and the tomboy is a brave girl who can hold her own with a boy her size. These attitudes probably become part of later attitudes toward homosexuality in the two sexes.

The attitude toward homosexuality in Western society may be summed up as follows: In most circles it is looked upon as an unacceptable form of sexual activity. When external circumstances make the attainment of a heterosexual choice temporarily or permanently impossible, as with women or with men in isolated situations, society is more tolerant of the homosexual situation. Also character traits usually associated with the homosexual affect the degree of disapproval of the individual invert. Thus the tomboy receives less contempt than the sissy.

People who for reasons external to their own personality find their choice of love object limited to their own sex may be said to be "normal" homosexuals, in the sense that they utilize the best types of interpersonal relationship available to them. These people are not the problem of psychopathology.

The question which concerns psychotherapists is what kind of inner difficulty predisposes a person to the choice of overt homosexuality as his preferred form of interpersonal relationship. When no external limitations are in evidence, is there any one predisposing factor or may it appear in a variety of interpersonal difficulties? Is it an outgrowth of a definite personality structure or do accidental factors add it to an already burdened personality? Or are there in each case definite tendencies from early childhood leading in the direction of homosexuality? It is possible that each of these situations may occur as a predisposing background, and that in each case the meaning of the symptom of homosexuality is determined by the background. In short, homosexuality is not a clinical entity, but a symptom with different meanings in different personality setups. One might compare its place in the neurosis to that of a headache in various diseases. A headache may be the result of brain tumor, a sinus, a beginning infectious disease, a migraine attack, an emotional disturbance, or a blow on the head. When the underlying disease is treated successfully, the headache disappears.

Similarly, overt homosexuality may express fear of the opposite sex, fear of adult responsibility, a need to defy authority, or an attempt to cope with hatred of or competitive attitudes to members of one's own sex; it may represent a flight from reality into absorption in body stimulation very similar to the autoerotic activities of the schizophrenic, or it may be a symptom of destructiveness of oneself or others. These do not exhaust the possibilities of its meaning. They merely represent situations which I have personally found in analyzing cases. The examples indicate the wide scope of difficulties which may find expression in the symptom.

The next concern is to determine if possible why this symptom is chosen as a solution of the difficulty. Can one invariably show in a given person tendencies which can clearly be traced from childhood, predisposing to homosexuality?

In many cases this seems to be true. In our culture, most children grow up in very close relationship to two people of opposite sexes. It is clear that a child has a distinct relationship to each parent and that sexual interest and curiosity play some part in this, although there are usually more important factors. The relationship is to a great extent molded by the role of that parent in the child's life. For example, the mother is usually more closely associated with the bodily needs than is the father. The father's function varies more widely. In some families he stands for discipline, in others he is the playmate, in others he shares the care of the child with the mother. These facts influence the child's reaction to the parent. In addition, the child has a relationship to the parent in terms of the kind of person the parent is. He early learns which parent wields the power, which loves him more, which is the more dependable, which one can be manipulated best by his techniques, and so on. These facts determine which parent the child prefers and where his allegiance lies. A very important determining influence in the development of homosexuality is the child's awareness that his sex was a disappointment to his parents or to the more important parent, especially if their disappointment leads them to treat the child as if he were of the opposite sex. However, none of these considerations invariably produce homosexuality in the adult. Girls whose parents wished them to be boys may grow up without any special interest in their own sex. Boys with gentle motherly qualities often marry and find satisfaction in mothering their own children without ever having gone through a struggle against homosexuality. If the father happened to be the strongest, most loving, and constructive influence in a boy's life and the mother failed him badly, the boy may become a homosexual, but it is equally probable he will seek a woman of his father's personality type; or if he is more seriously damaged, he will be driven to marry a woman with a destructive influence on him somewhat in the pattern of his mother, or he may even become involved in a homosexual relation with a destructive man. In the same manner one can take up all the possible personality combinations found in parents and show that they in themselves do not predetermine the choice of the sex of the later partner.

Sexual relationships seem to be determined along two main lines. There is the constructive choice where mutual helpfulness and affection dominate the picture, and there is the destructive choice where one finds himself bound to the person whom he fears and who may destroy him—the moth and flame fascination. There are of course many in-between situations where, for example, the partnership is on the whole constructive but has some destructive elements, and so on. This distinction cuts across sex lines. There are both types of heterosexual relationships and both types of homosexual ones.

It is therefore necessary to look further for definite predetermining factors in the formation of the symptom of homosexuality. Two other considerations are important in this respect—the degree of personality damage and the role of accidental factors. People who have been greatly intimidated or have a low self-esteem and therefore have difficulties in making friends and being comfortable with other people have a tendency to cling to their own sex because it is less frightening. They feel understood by people like themselves. There is not the terrifying unpredictability of the unknown. Moreover, relationship with the opposite sex makes greater demands—the man is expected to support the woman, a woman is expected to have children. Also the frightened woman fears to test whether she is sufficiently attractive to win a man, and the frightened man fears he may not be sufficiently successful to attract a woman. However, the above considerations do not invariably produce homosexuality, for the fear of disapproval from the culture and the need to conform often drive these very people into marriage. The fact that one is married by no means proves that one is a mature person.

A homosexual way of life also attracts people who fear intimacy and yet are equally afraid of loneliness. As already mentioned, one's own sex is less frightening because it is familiar. The relationship looks less permanent, less entrapping, as if one could get away at any time. To be sure, the appearance of freedom often proves deceptive, for neurotic attachments with either sex have a way of becoming binding through neurotic dependencies. Among men the fear of the struggle for existence tempts a certain number to become dependent financially as well as otherwise on another man.

Thus far I have shown that various personality problems may find partial solution in a homosexual symptom, but nothing has been shown as specifically producing homosexuality. Some writers have laid great stress on the importance of early seduction by homosexuals, and many homosexuals attribute their way of life to such experiences. However, many people have such experiences without becoming homosexual. It is probable that a homosexual experience to a boy who is already heavily burdened, fears women, and feels unequal to life may add the decisive last touch to his choice of neurosis. Yet a similar seduction of a boy not afraid of life is but an incident in the process of investigation of life, and he simply goes on to master new experiences. Homosexual play is known to be very frequent in preadolescence and causes no serious disturbance in the majority of children.

Perhaps because of Freud's great emphasis on the sexual origin of neurosis and perhaps also because of the strong cultural disapproval, therapists are likely to think of homosexuality as a more fundamentally significant symptom than it really is. It seems certain from analysis in recent years that it is a problem which tends to disappear when the general character problems are solved.

Even as a symptom, homosexuality does not present a uniform appearance. There are at least as many different types of homosexual behavior as of heterosexual, and the interpersonal relations of homosexuals present the same problems as are found in heterosexual situations. So the mother-child attachment is sometimes found to be the important part of the picture. Frequently competitive and sadomasochistic feelings dominate the union. There are relationships based on hatred and fear and also relationships of mutual helpfulness. Promiscuity is possibly more frequent among homosexuals than heterosexuals, but its significance in the personality structure is very similar in the two. In both the chief interest is in genitals and body stimulation. The person chosen to share the experience is not important. The sexual activity is compulsive and is the sole interest. In fact in much activity carried on in movies, the partner is not even clearly seen and often not a word is exchanged.

At the other extreme is the homosexual marriage, by which I mean a relatively durable, long-term relationship between two people—a relationship in which the interests and personalities of each are important to the other. Here again we may find all of the pictures of a neurotic heterosexual marriage, the same possessiveness, jealousies, and struggles for power. The idea may be at least theoretically entertained that a homosexual adult love relationship can exist. Adult love seems to be a rare experience in our culture anyway and would doubtless be even more rare among homosexuals, because a person with the necessary degree of maturity would probably prefer a heterosexual relation unless external circumstances in his life made this impossible.

So the actual choice of homosexuality as the preferred form of interpersonal relations may have different origins in different cases, as I have indicated. If it is caused by some one specific situation or combination of circumstances, that has not yet been discovered.

Even though the specific cause for homosexuality cannot be found, the specific needs which it satisfies can be examined. Obviously it gives sexual satisfaction, and for a person unable to make contact with the opposite sex, this is important. Also, because it requires a partner, it helps cope with the problem of loneliness and isolation. The very fact of belonging to a culturally taboo group has its satisfactions. One can feel defiant, brave, and strong, and as a member of a band united against the world, lessen the feeling of ostracism. I have spoken earlier of other satisfactions, such as financial support—especially in the case of some male homosexuals—and freedom from responsibility.

An overt homosexual way of life can play a constructive or destructive role in the personality. It may be the best type of human relation of which a person is capable and as such is better than isolation. This would apply especially to the mother-child type of dependencies found in homosexuals of both sexes. Or it may be an added destructive touch in a deteriorating personality. In no case will it be found to be the cause of the rest of the neurotic structure—the basic origin of the neurosis—although after it is established, it may contribute to the problems. As in the case of other symptoms in neurosis, psychoanalysis must deal primarily with the personality structure realizing that the symptom is a secondary development from that.

Role of Women in This Culture

When Freud first wrote his *Studies in Hysteria*** in the 1890's, he described a type of woman with ambitions and prospects very different from those found in the average psychoanalytic patient of today. That a radical change has occurred is partly due to Freud's own efforts in clarifying the whole question of the sexual life, but largely due to changes in the economic and social status of women. These changes were already occurring before the time of Freud.[2]

In this country today women occupy a unique position. They are probably freer to live their own lives than in any patriarchal country in the world. This does not mean that they have ceased to be an underprivileged group. They are discriminated against in many situations without regard for their needs or ability. One would expect, therefore, to find the reality situation bringing out inferiority feelings not only because of a reaction to the immediate situation but because of family teaching in childhood based on the same cultural attitude. One would expect to find, also very frequently, resentment toward men because of their privileged position, as if the men themselves were

---

* Sigmund Freud, *Studies in Hysteria* (New York: Basic Books, Inc., 1957).

[2] Notes and References, pp. 179–182.

to blame for this. These are some of the more important factors that contribute to a woman's feeling of inferiority.

As we know, the culture of Europe and America has been based for centuries on a patriarchal system. In this system, exclusive ownership of the female by a given male is important. One of the results has been the relegating of women to the status of property without a voice in their own fate. To be sure, there have always been women who, by their cleverness or special circumstances, have been able to circumvent this position, but in general, the girl child has been trained from childhood to fit herself for her inferior role; and, as long as compensations were adequate, women have been relatively content. For example, if in return for being a man's property a woman receives economic security, a full emotional life centering around husband and children, and an opportunity to express her capacities in the management of her home, she has little cause for discontent. The question of her inferiority scarcely troubles her when her life is happily fulfilled, even though she lives in relative slavery. If, therefore, the problem of women today simply referred to their position in a patriarchal culture, the task would be much simpler. However, without considering the fact that the individual husband may be unsatisfactory and so produce discontent, other factors are also at work to create dissatisfaction. As Erich Fromm has said, "When a positive gain of a culture begins to fail, then restlessness comes until a new satisfaction is found." Our problem with women today is not simply that they are caught in a patriarchal culture, but that they are living in a culture in which the positive gains for them are failing.

Industry has been taken out of the home. Large families are no longer desired or economically possible. Also, other more emotionally tinged factors contribute to the housewife's dissatisfaction. The home is no longer the center of the husband's life. If one adds to this the fact that the sexual life is often still dominated by puritanical ideas, the position of the present-day wife who tries to live in the traditional manner cannot but be one with a constant narrowing of interests and possibilities for development. Increasingly, the woman finds herself without an occupation and with an unsatisfactory emotional life.

On the other hand, the culture is beginning to offer her something positive in an opportunity to join in a life outside the home where she may compete with other women and even with men in business. In the sexual sphere, too, with the spread of birth-control knowledge and a more open attitude in general about sex, there is an increasing tendency in and out of marriage to have a sexual life approximating in its freedom that enjoyed by the male. However, these things do not yet run smoothly. In other words, we are not yet dealing with a stable situation, but one in transition; therefore, one in which the individual is confused and filled with conflict, one in which old attitudes and training struggle with new ideas.

Woman's restlessness began to make itself felt about the middle of the last century. Prior to that and even for some time afterward, the position of woman was fairly clear-cut and stable. Her training was directed toward marriage and motherhood. If she made a good marriage, she was a success. If she made a bad marriage, she must try to adjust to it because it was almost impossible to escape. If she made no marriage, she was doomed to a life of frustration. Not only was sexual satisfaction denied her but she felt herself branded a failure who must live on sufferance in the home of her parents, or of a brother or sister, where she might have a meager emotional life from the love of other people's children. Not only must she suffer actual disappointment, but she had the additional burden of inferiority feelings. She had failed to achieve the goal demanded by the culture—and for women there was only one goal.

There were a few exceptions. For instance, the Brontës, although leading very frustrated lives, at least were able to develop their gifts and to achieve success. But work and the professions were for the most part closed to women. If one's own family could not provide for an unmarried woman, she might find a home as governess or teacher in some other family. However, there were occasional daring women. As early as 1850 a woman had "crashed" the medical profession. She was considered a freak and accused of immorality. She had to face insults and gibes from her colleagues. Very slowly the number of woman physicians increased. Still later, they entered the other professions and business. On the whole, the number of women who in one way or another became independent of their families before 1900 was small. World War I speeded the process and gave the stamp of social approval to economic independence for woman. Since then, she has been able to enter almost every field of work for which she is physically capable, but even yet she is seldom accepted on equal terms with men.

Many interesting factors are revealed in this new situation of women. In the first place they are young in their present role. Comparatively few of them have the background of mothers or grandmothers who engaged in any work outside the home. They have to work out a new way of life with no precedent to follow and no adequate training from early childhood to help them take the work drive seriously or fit it into their lives. It is not strange that the outstanding successes are few and that the great majority of women effect some compromise between the old and the new. For instance, the majority still plan to work only until they marry.* This is true not only of the relatively unskilled worker but often of the highly trained. This may mean that the young woman not only does not do her premarital job well and in a way to give her satisfaction, but also nothing in her premarriage activity is helpful in fitting her for the business of homemaker.

Second, even when the individual has the courage in herself to attempt the new road, she has to cope with emotional pressures not only from society as a whole but from the individuals most important to her. One of the most significant of these pressures is the attitude of

* [Written in 1941—Ed.]

a prospective husband who has his own traditions and wishes for his future wife and, since he is often confused in his attempt to adjust to the new ways of life, may interpret the woman's struggle to find a place for herself as evidence of lack of love or a slur on his manhood.[8]

Even the attitude of parents is often far from constructive. They do not have as great an emotional stake in a daughter's business success as in that of a son, and they are less likely to make sacrifices for her career. Sometimes they actually oppose it.

Because so many of the child's ideals are modeled on attitudes of the parents, the girl may be further handicapped by incongruities built into her own ego. For example, a young woman brought up in a Southern home, where nothing was expected of woman except to be charming, found herself in adult life in a profession where she must compete to hold her own. Both healthy and neurotic factors had driven her from her parents' adjustment. Her superior intelligence had stimulated her to go far in education, and lack of social ease— rising out of physical inferiority feelings—had reenforced this drive. Nevertheless, her ways of adjustment were definitely modeled on her past. Although she was in a position where she should be a leader with definite views and initiative to execute them, she was constantly deferring to men, seeking to flatter them by playing the yielding, clinging vine, accepting their advice even when she thought differently. Her conscious desire to be a modern woman led her to pretend to herself that she did not want to marry. To prove it she had several extramarital sexual affairs but in them she was frigid. She constantly felt humiliated because she had not achieved the traditional goal of marriage.

This example serves to show how the inconsistencies and conflicts—rising when a cultural situation is in a state of rapid transition—become a part of the neurotic conflict of the individual, even as they influence the form of the neurotic behavior.

Finally, social institutions put obstacles in the way of change of a woman's status. In the economic sphere she must usually accept a lower wage than men for the same type of work. She must usually be more capable than the man with whom she competes before she will be considered his equal.

Even with increased economic freedom, there is considerable variation in the social satisfactions available to independent women. In some groups any type of relationship with men or women is open to the woman who is emotionally able to accept it. In other groups a woman's social life may be even more restricted than it was in the days when she was overprotected in the home. In the latter groups, unless she shows great initiative in changing her situation, she may find herself forced to associate entirely with her own sex. While this is in itself a great cause for discontent, many individuals find a more or less satisfactory solution for its limitations, while others find neurotic security in the manless world. Thus it is possible for a woman teaching in a girls' school to reach the age of forty still living fairly happily on an adolescent "crush" level.

Whatever the problems created in the new life of woman, her status must continue to change, for she is being driven out of the home by her restlessness due in part at least to her lack of occupation. The life of the married woman today who has no special work interest is not exciting. She has a small home, or in many cases only a small apartment. She may have no children; she may have at most three. Even if she does her own housework it is so simplified by modern inventions that it can fill only a few hours of her day. Because of the nature of modern business life she often has very little share in her husband's interests. What can she do? She may make a cult of her child, or she may play bridge or have some other play life, or she may engage in some volunteer employment—in which she is apt to be no longer welcome since trained workers are increasingly preferred—or she may go to work seriously. The last solution is growing in popularity.

Let us consider three frequently encountered types

of reaction to the current situation: women who marry and try to live according to the old pattern but find themselves unemployed and often discontented; women who work and do not marry; and, women who marry and engage in serious work outside the home.

The first group, those who marry and have no other work interest, is a very large group. It often happens that intelligent and capable women find themselves in this situation because they had not been aware of the reality before marriage and no preparation for any other type of life had been made. That is, these individuals had married with the fantasy that life after marriage could be lived somewhat in the old-fashioned way according to the pattern of the home life of their childhood. Many college women are in this group; especially college women who married immediately after graduation and did not fit themselves for any profession or work. Making a cult of the child is unfortunately a fairly frequent solution. By the term *cult* is here meant an anxious concern about the child's welfare where the mother goes to excessive lengths to apply all modern psychological and hygienic theories to the management of her child's development. This can be very destructive for the child.

Another type of woman finds in the marriage with no responsibility the fulfillment of her neurotic needs. This is the very infantile woman. For her marriage is a kind of sanitarium life. She often shirks childbearing and in her relationship to her husband she has the position of spoiled child. Many of these women could not survive outside the protected atmosphere of their marriages.

Of the second group, those who work and do not marry, there are two main subdivisions. First, there are those to whom work is everything; that is, there is no love life of significance. This woman differs from her predecessor, the old maid, in that she is economically independent. She may, however, be even more miserable because her life is often very isolated, whereas the old maid of the past generation usually lived in a family and had a kind of vicarious life. Many of these individuals do find some kind of sublimated satisfaction, for example, working for some cause even as their predecessors worked for religion. This group might be characterized as having found economic freedom without emotional freedom.

The second group are those who have a love life in addition to work. This love life may be homosexual or heterosexual, and the relationships may vary from the casual with frequent changes of partner to a fairly permanent relationship with one person, a relationship which may differ very little from marriage. In all of them, however, there is one important difference from a married partnership. The individual considers herself free although she actually may be very involved emotionally. She regards her work as the most important and permanent thing in her life.

In the group who marry and engage in work outside the home, several possibilities of relationship exist. Husband and wife may continue to lead independent business lives. They may be interested in each other's work without being competitive in any way. There may be real enjoyment in the success of the other. This is the ideal situation. It is more likely to work when the two are engaged in different types of occupation.

The husband's resentment and competitive attitude may crush the wife's initiative, a situation which was more frequent a few years ago. The man feels that his virility is threatened. He fears that people will think he cannot support her or he fears that he will lose his power over her, and so forth. In such situations, if the marriage continues, the wife must give up her work—often without any adequate interest to take its place.

The wife who proves to be the better breadwinner may win out in the competition, especially since the depression. This is culturally a most revolutionary situation; it can make a great many difficulties. The woman needs extraordinary tact in handling it. If under the influence of her own cultural training she feels contempt for the husband or a desire to rub it in, matters can become very bad. In general, the man needs some face-saving explanation. He cannot say that he prefers to keep house, even when, occasionally, this is the case. He could not accept it himself, and most of his acquaintances would think less of him for it. So, he has to be unable to get work and, therefore, keeps house to help his wife who is working, or he must be ill, or he must be getting an education, in all of which cases he is able to accept his wife's economic support without loss of self-respect.

Thus far we have said almost nothing about child-bearing. What has become of this important biologic function in our culture? In the present economic situation in the United States increase of population is not desired. The fact that small families are the rule is one of the factors driving women out of the home. Now that they are out of the home a kind of vicious circle is formed, for it is no longer convenient to be occupied in the home by one or two children. Much conflict centers here, for it is one of the problems of the culture which as yet has no generally satisfactory solution. Individual women have worked out ways of having both children and a career, but most women still do the one or the other; and in either case there are regrets and often neurotic discontent. The business or professional woman who had decided against children, consciously or unconsciously, does not want them; her difficulty arises from the fact that she often cannot admit this to herself. Perhaps some biologic yearning disturbs her, or some desire to have all of life's experiences, or perhaps there is merely the influence of the traditional cultural pattern which might be expressed thus: "A woman is expected to want a child." She may thus feel it her duty to prove her adequacy as a woman by having a child. She may resist, devote herself to her career, but it bothers her and makes her feel inferior. On the other hand, the problem is not solved by going to the other extreme and trying to prove one's adequacy as a woman by having a child or two. The women of past generations had no choice but to bear children. Since their lives were organized around this concept of duty, they seldom became aware of dislike of the situation, but there must have been many unwanted children then.

* * *

Let us glance at the picture which Freud first described early in the 1890's. Young women of good family grew up apparently in sexual ignorance; they were allowed no legitimate opportunity to gratify their sexual curiosity in theory or in fact. At puberty they entered a life of severe restrictions by which an artificial form of behavior was fostered. Further general education was discouraged and, while on the one hand they were to show no interest in sex in any form, they at the same time must devote their lives to getting husbands. This situation must have led to profound confusion in the mind of many an adolescent girl. She knew she must marry, bear children, but never admit that she enjoyed sex. Certainly, adjustment was achieved by the women of that generation at great emotional cost. Freud's first insights about the importance of the sexual life and its significance in neurosis arose in such an atmosphere, at the very time women were beginning to be pushed out of the home. The fiction of purity, chastity, and innocence was becoming increasingly difficult to maintain. Reality pressures, in which Freud's discoveries had no small part, were making adequate sexual information more important. A greater frankness and sincerity about the sexual life was coming about. The problem could no longer be handled by overprotection and ignorance. As a result, the pendulum was swinging toward the revolt against all restraint which became manifest in the United States between 1920 and 1930. It then appeared not only that women were realizing their legitimate sexual stake in marriage, but even high-school girls felt a necessity for sexual episodes to herald in a rebellious way the coming of the new freedom. One of them, a patient, in comparing the old and the new, said, "Men used to think they had to pay a woman. Now they've discovered that the girls like it too." At any rate, escaping from chaperones, going into industry—in other words, leaving the protected conventlike atmosphere of the Victorian era—women found themselves overwhelmed with new emotional problems for which they had even less preparation than they had for the economic changes. Sexual freedom resulted, but in many cases the freedom was not without expense. The woman in trying to overthrow her early training was unable to get her own consent, as it were, and found herself frigid. The reverse swing of the pendulum appeared in the 1930's. While it may swing far back under the influence of fascism, war may result in another forward thrust.

It is difficult to portray the sexual attitude of today's women. There are many different, often half-digested, attitudes. The culture still leans to the conservative side. The tendency is still to expect the woman to confine her sexual life to her marriage partner. Children born out of wedlock are still stigmatized in some groups, though certainly with nothing like the ferocity of fifty years ago. One still may encounter as a patient a woman who feels she can never get over the disgrace of having been pregnant two months before her marriage. While most of one's female patients accept sexual life out of marriage as a matter of course, many of them are unwilling to defy the culture to the extent of bearing children. Absence of virginity at the time of marriage is no longer a universal cause for dismay but it can still be disturbing to some people. In but few groups can the woman openly acknowledge that she has a lover. In general, she must be more secretive than is a man. In brief, in many situations today, a woman may have any kind of sexual life that she wishes if, and only if, she does not make herself conspicuous.

One result of these circumstances seems inevitable: Marriage becomes much less important than it was. A woman once needed it as a means of economic support as well as a source of sexual satisfaction. Both factors have shrunk in importance. The companionship of marriage can conceivably be found in other situations;

no satisfactory substitute has yet appeared to satisfy the economic and emotional needs of children.

The official attitude of the culture then is conservative but the practical attitude in certain groups is radical. The best examples of the latter are found in the group of women who work and have a sexual life outside of marriage, although the same types of behavior can also be seen in some married women. As suggested above, nominal freedom of behavior does not necessarily indicate inner freedom from conflict. Many women avail themselves of sexual opportunities, but cannot rid themselves of a sense of guilt arising from old ideas; or the sense of guilt may be repressed and in its place may come frigidity—a denying that the act is taking place—promiscuity as a kind of defiance of the inner prohibition, or other compromise behavior. Moreover, sexual freedom can be an excellent instrument for the expression of neurotic drives arising outside the strictly sexual sphere, especially drives expressive of hostility to men, or of the desire to be a man. Thus promiscuity may mean the collecting of scalps with the hope of hurting men, frustrating them, or taking away their importance, or in another case it may mean to the woman that she is herself a man. For example, a young woman whose business life threw her into sharp competition with men was proud of the fact that she acted like a man in her sexual life. She had a series of lovers to no one of whom she allowed herself to become attached. If she found herself becoming involved, she was upset until she had succeeded in discarding the man in such a way that he would conclude that she had no interest in him. This to her mind was acting like a man; permitting an emotional attachment to develop would have been acting like a woman.

It is then apparent that while the sexual emancipation of women may be a step forward in personality development for some, it may only offer a new means for neurotic expression to others.

Overt homosexuality among women is probably more frequent at the present time than formerly. The diminishing emphasis on marriage and children helps to bring it to the fore, and the social isolation from men that now characterizes some types of work must be an encouragement to any homosexual tendencies which exist. It seems that many women who would otherwise never give overt expression to these tendencies are driven together by loneliness, and in their living together all degrees of intimacy are found. The culture seems to be decidedly more tolerant of these relationships between women than of similar ones between men.

The question that is raised in any study of change, whether by evolution or revolution, takes the form: Can one say that people are more benefited or harmed? Have our women actually solved any of their problems in the last fifty years? When Freud analyzed his first cases, he described some of the basic conflicts which we still encounter, albeit the emphasis is different. Then, the young girl who might wish to be a boy could only give symbolic expression to this in the form of hysterical fantasies. Today, she may live out the fantasy, at least in part. In her business relations and in her sexual relations she may act in many ways like a man. Many a woman with severe personality difficulties uses the new opportunities provided by the culture for neurotic purposes without much benefit except that in so doing she is able to be a "going concern." On the other hand, many women use the present-day situation more constructively. As they acquire more freedom to express their capacities and emotional needs, they find less actual reason to envy the male. The handicap of being a woman is, culturally speaking, not as great now as it was fifty years ago.[4]

Inevitably, poorly adjusted people are in the vanguard of revolutionary movements. This one for the emancipation of women is certainly no exception. Women who studied medicine in the early years were on the whole those who had great personal problems about being women. Many a parallel example readily comes to mind. Some therapists may carry the marks of experience in those days. In any case, there is a temptation to view all change as neurotic. This obviously is an extreme stand. Neurotic drives often find expression in the present-day activities of women, but this is no reason for dismissing as neurotic the whole social and economic revolution of woman along her particular path among the worldwide changes.

Cultural Pressures in the Psychology of Women

The importance of cultural influences in personality problems has become more and more significant in psychoanalytic work. A given culture tends to produce certain types of character. In *The Neurotic Personality of Our Time** Karen Horney has described well certain trends found in this culture. Most of these neurotic trends are found working similarly in both sexes. Thus, for example, the so-called masochistic character is by no means an exclusively feminine phenomenon. Likewise the neurotic need to be loved is often found dominating the life of men as well as women. The neurotic need of power and insatiable ambition drives are not only found in men, but also in women.

Nevertheless, in some respects the problems of women are basically different from those of men. These fundamental differences are due to two things. First, woman has a different biologic function and because of this her position in society necessarily differs in some respects from that of the man. Second, the cultural attitude toward women differs significantly from that

* Karen Horney, *The Neurotic Personality of Our Time* (New York: W. W. Norton, 1937).

toward men for reasons quite apart from biological necessity. These two differences present women with certain problems which men do not have to face.

The biologic problems of a woman's life cannot be ignored, although it would seem that in most cases biology becomes a problem chiefly when it produces a situation which is unsatisfactory in the cultural setup. Menstruation, pregnancy, and the menopause can bring to a woman certain hazards of which there is no comparable difficulty in the male biology. Freud was so impressed with the biologic difficulties of woman that, as is well known, he believed all inferiority feelings of woman had their root in her biologic inadequacies. To say that a woman has to encounter certain hazards that a man does not, does not seem to be the same thing as saying woman is biologically inferior, as Freud implies.

* * *

According to Freud, because of the little girl's discovery that she has no penis she enters the Oedipus complex with castration already an accomplished fact, while in the little boy the threat of castration arises as a result of the Oedipus complex and brings about its repression. Out of this situation in the little boy Freud believes much that is important in the superego takes its origin. Since the little girl, feeling herself already castrated, need fear no further threat she has less tendency to repress her Oedipus complex and less tendency to develop a superego.

Furthermore, according to Freud, one fact which reinforces the high evaluation of the penis by the little girl is that she is at the time of its discovery unaware that she has a vagina. She therefore considers her clitoris her sole sexual apparatus and is exclusively interested in it throughout childhood. Since she believes this is all she has in place of a penis this emphasizes her inferiority. In addition, the ignorance of the vagina makes for her a special hazard at puberty because the onset of menstruation brings awareness of her female role and requires her to give up her interest in the clitoris and henceforth to seek sexual satisfaction by way of the vagina. With this comes a change in her character. She gives up her boyish aggressiveness and becomes femininely passive.

These are the highlights of the more strictly biologic aspects of Freud's theory of the development of women. I shall touch presently on some other details, but now I wish to review the gross outline in the light of my first consideration, the problem aspect of the biology of woman. The question must be asked: Is this the true story of the biologic sexual development of women? Penis envy dating from an experience in early childhood is sometimes recalled by women patients. In my experience, however, this memory is not recalled by all patients—not even by all of those who present in other respects the clinical picture of penis envy. While a negative finding is not conclusive it suggests that other factors may also contribute to envy of the male. Also, quite frequently, one finds women patients who are not aware of the clitoris as a separate organ and learned it only later in studying biology. This was true even though they had exploited the pleasurable sensations in the region of the clitoris. Although ignorance of the vagina, sometimes until far into adolescence, has been observed especially in hysterics, equally often one finds knowledge of the vagina from an early age and often a history of vaginal masturbation. These facts certainly cast doubt on the idea that the clitoris is always the center of the little girl's interest. It seems that one is in fact entitled to question whether there is, even now, any adequate information concerning the innate sexual interests of women.

However, Freud was usually a keen clinical observer and it may therefore be assumed that his theory was based upon certain facts which he observed. The probable nature of these facts and the principal sources of error in his interpretation of the observations may be considered.

Of the latter, there seem to have been two. In the first place, he saw the problem entirely from a masculine point of view. Horney draws attention to this in her paper "Flight from Womanhood,"* published in 1926. In it she marshals data to show that the attitude prevalent in the male about his own genitals was accepted by Freud as the attitude of both sexes on the matter. She indicates that Freud based his theory on the assumption that the penis is the sexual organ most highly valued by both sexes and at no point in his work showed any recognition of the possibility of there being a female biologic function in its own right. He saw the woman primarily as the negative of the male. The most extreme example of this appears in his theory that woman accepts her ability to produce a child as a compensation for her lack of a penis. Childbearing is a sufficiently important biologic function to have value for its own sake. Surely, only a man could have thought of it in terms of compensation or consolation.

The second source of error in Freud's thinking is the fact that he studied only women in his own or closely related cultures, that because he had no comparative study of other cultures he believed that what he observed was universal woman. Current studies show that this is clearly not the case.

The women observed by psychoanalysts are distinctly women living in a particular culture, the Western culture, a patriarchal culture in a state of transition. It is impossible to separate from the total picture something which one can safely call biologic woman. It is assumed that she exists, that she has her reactions to her particular organic make-up, but it is increasingly clear that not all that seems biologic is biologic. That women behave differently in different types of culture is now beginning to be known, although intensive analyses of women in other cultures have not yet been made. Freud, ignoring these considerations, thought the attitudes, interests, and ambitions of the middle- and upper-class women whom he analyzed to be the characteristic attitudes, interests, and ambitions of women in general.

* Karen Horney, "Flight from Womanhood," *International Journal of Psycho-Analysis*, VII (1926), 324–339.

Today one realizes that much which even woman herself may attribute to the fact of her sex can be explained as the result of cultural pressures. At the same time, the fact that bearing children must influence women's personality development cannot be denied. Also the type of sexual response characteristic of a woman conceivably has its influence on her character.

For example, it seems probable that the very fact that the male must achieve an erection in order to carry out the sexual act and that any failure in this attempt cannot be hidden while the female can much more readily hide her success or nonsuccess in intercourse, may well have an effect in the basic character patterns of both. Even here, however, more complete understanding of the cultural pressures is necessary before it can be stated in what way or to what extent biology plays a part. But one thing seems fairly certain; namely, that to the extent to which a woman is biologically fulfilled—whatever that may mean—to that extent she has no tendency to envy man's biology, or to feel inferior about her biologic make-up.

In certain cultures woman can meet with difficulties which would make her biologic make-up appear to be a handicap. This would be true when her drives are denied expression or when fulfillment of the role of woman puts her at a disadvantage. Both of these situations are true in many respects in the United States today. This is essentially a patriarchal culture and although many values are changing and these changes on the whole are working to the advantage of women, the patriarchal situation still presents limitations to a woman's free development of her interests. Also, the newer situations have their hazards in that they usually throw women into unequal competition with men. By unequal, the reference is not to biologic inequality, but an inequality resulting from prejudice and the greater advantages offered the male.

The official attitude of the culture toward women has been and still is to the effect that woman is not the equal of man. This has led to the following things: Until very recently woman was not offered education even

approximately equal to that given a man; when she did
secure reasonably adequate education, she found more
limited opportunities for using the training than did a
man; woman was considered helpless, partly because
she was not given an opportunity to work, and partly
because she had no choice but to be economically
dependent on some man; and social restrictions were
placed on her, especially in connection with her sex
life. These restrictions seemed to work to the advantage
of the man.

The assumption of woman's inferiority was a part of
the prevalent attitude of society and until very recently
was accepted by both sexes as a biologic fact. Since
there is obvious advantage to the male in believing this,
he has proved much more resistant to a new point of
view on the matter than have women. Women, at the
same time, have had difficulty in freeing themselves
from an idea which was a part of their life training.
Thus it has come about that even when a woman has
become consciously convinced of her value she still has
to contend with the unconscious effects of training,
discrimination against her, and traumatic experiences
which keep alive the attitude of inferiority.

The women whom Freud observed were women in
this situation and it was easy for him to generalize the
effects of the attitude of the culture as a fact of biology.

It seems justifiable therefore not only to consider
Freud's theory in the light of his masculine bias but to
examine closely the particular cultural pressures which
may have produced the picture of woman as he saw
her.

He found that the central problem in the neurotic
difficulties of most women was penis envy. If this is
interpreted symbolically it will be agreed that in this
culture where the advantages go to the possessor of the
penis women often find themselves in situations which
arouse their envy of men, and so, in their relations to
men, they show an attitude which can be called "penis
envy."

An awareness of the advantage of a penis might be
vaguely conscious in a little girl's mind at the age of

three—for already at that age evidences that the son is more privileged are apparent in many middle-class families. Before one can settle the question of whether this early experience takes place in terms of actual envy of the penis, or whether the boy is envied in a more general way, it must be noticed that until very recently the average girl at puberty was made decidedly aware of the disadvantages of being female. In the Victorian era the transition from the freedom of childhood to the restrictions of adolescence must have been especially conducive of unhappiness. An experience of a patient as recently as fifteen years ago shows vividly the still existing cultural situation. Two children, a boy and a girl, the boy a year and a half older than the girl, grew up in a family where freedom of development was encouraged. They were both very fond of outdoor life, and went on long hikes together, often camping out overnight. At the age of twelve suddenly a great change was introduced into the girl's life. She was told that now since she was about to become a woman she could no longer go away with her brother on overnight trips. This was only one evidence, but one very important to her, of the beginning limitation of her activities. She was filled with bitterness and envy of her brother and for several reasons centered her whole resentment on the fact of menstruation. This seemed to her to be the sign of her disgrace, the sign that she had no right to be a person. She became withdrawn and depressed. Her one strong feeling was that she hated to be a woman and did not want to grow up. The condition developed decisively because of the restrictions of adolescence, restrictions which actually changed her whole way of life. I do not wish to imply that this pathologic reaction to the situation at puberty developed in a hitherto healthy girl. Envy of her brother had existed in child-hood because of her mother's marked preference for him, but a long period of equality with him had done much to restore her self-esteem. The situation at puberty re-established the idea that he was the more favored person.

The changes brought about by cultural restrictions at

the girl's puberty are not of a superficial nature. At this time in the Victorian picture a girl passed from a position of relative equality with boys to one of inferiority. This inferiority was shown in several ways. An outstanding point of the picture was the inhibition of natural aggression. A girl might no longer make demands and go about freely. If she was interested in a boy she must not show it directly. She must never expose herself to possible rejection. This would mean she had been unwomanly. She might no longer pursue her own interests with the same freedom as a boy. Obstacles were placed in the way of her education, her play, and social life. But especially in her sexual life her freedom of development was curbed. The punishment for spontaneous expression of sexual interests was very great. One impulsive act resulting in pregnancy could ruin a girl's whole life. Her training was in the direction of insincerity about her sexual interests. She was taught to be ashamed of menstruation. It was something to be concealed and any accident leading to its discovery was especially humiliating. In short, womanhood began with much unpleasantness. It was characterized by feelings of body shame, loss of freedom, loss of equality with boys, and loss of the right to be aggressive. The training in insincerity, especially about her sexual being and sexual interests, has undoubtedly contributed much to a woman's diminished sense of self. When something so vitally a part of her must be denied it is not a great step further to deny the whole self. The fact that much of this has noticeably changed in the last fifty years seems sufficient proof that this situation was due to a cultural attitude and had nothing to do with innate femininity. Freud, observing this cultural change in the girl's status at puberty, attributed it to the necessity of accepting her feminine passivity, which he said she could not do without a struggle. Is it not more accurate to say that at puberty it became necessary for the girl to accept the restrictions placed on women, and that this was usually unwelcome? In a word, the difficulties of adjustment found in the girl at puberty are the results of social pressures and do not arise from the difficulty of giving up the clitoris in favor of the vagina.

The cultural attitude about the sexual life of women has been one of denial. In former years there was denial almost of its very existence. Today there is still some tendency to deny that it is as important or urgent as the sexual life of men. Passivity and masochism are usually considered essential characteristics of a woman's sexual drive. Passivity was clearly forced upon her by the inhibition of the right to aggression. Her masochism also often proves to be a form of adaptation to an unsatisfactory and circumscribed life.

Not only in her sexual life has the woman had reason to envy the man. The circumscribing of her intellectual development and the discouragement of personal initiative have been frustrating. Partly from lack of training and partly because of man's desire for ownership woman has had to accept a position of economic dependence on man, and this is still the rule.

Out of this situation come several personality traits which are generally considered typically feminine and which have even been described in psychoanalytic literature as the outcome of woman's biologic make-up. Women are supposed to be more narcissistic than men, to have a greater need to be loved than men, to be more rigid than men, and to have weaker superegos than men, these in addition to the already mentioned attitudes of passivity and masochism.

A review of the actual position of economic helplessness of women of the recent past and the relative economic helplessness of many women today leads one to question the innateness of these personality traits. The function of childbearing cannot but have some effect on the personality of woman, but when this function is accompanied by the necessity to legalize the process by marriage and economic dependency—with the only alternative social ostracism and added difficulties in the economic sphere if she does not marry—one cannot help thinking that woman's greater need to be loved and to have one meaningful sexual relation rather than the more casual sexual life of the man comes about chiefly because she lives in a culture which provides no security for her except a permanent so-called love relationship. It is known that the neurotic need of love is a mechanism for establishing security in a dependency relation. In the same way to the extent that a woman has a greater need of love than a man it is also to be interpreted as a device for establishing security in a cultural situation producing dependency. Being loved not only is part of woman's natural life in the same way as it is part of man's but it also becomes of necessity her profession. Making her body sexually attractive and her personality seductive is imperative for purposes of security. In the past centuries she could feel safe after she had married and could then risk neglecting her charms, but today, with the present ease of divorce, the woman who depends on a man for her means of support and social position must continue to devote a great deal of her time to what may be called narcissistic pursuits, that is, body culture and concern about clothes. One sees that woman's alleged narcissism and greater need to be loved may be entirely the result of economic necessity.

The idea that women must have weaker superegos than men, as stated by Freud, derives from the notion that in the little girl the Oedipus complex is usually not repressed. Because she enters the Oedipus phase after accepting the fact of castration she has no fear to drive her to repression and the formation of a superego. Not only Freud but other writers, notably Sachs, have pointed out that women therefore often lack strong convictions, strong consciences, but rather tend to take on the convictions and standards of any men on whom they become dependent in the course of their lives. This is said to be especially noticeable in women who have loved several men. Such a woman is supposed to adopt in succession the attitudes of the various men.

Undoubtedly there are many women who answer this description, but the character trait of having no strong beliefs or convictions is not found universally in women and also occurs frequently in men in this culture.

It is an attitude typical of people who have found

that their security depends on approval of some powerful person or group. It is relatively easy to become converted to any ideology which will bring one advantage, especially if one has never for neurotic or reality reasons been able to achieve sufficient independence to be able to know one's own mind. This could scarcely but be the case with the Victorian girl who was not permitted to free herself from her father until she was safely entrusted to the protection of another man. For cultural reasons, the girl had to continue to be dependent on her father and emancipation from the childhood tie was not encouraged. Such a situation is not conducive to the development of independent standards. That some women despite this became independent is remarkable.

One other statement of Freud's requires consideration: the idea that women are more rigid than men and lose their capacity for intellectual and emotional growth earlier. He points to the fact that a woman of thirty often seems already incapable of further development while a man of the same age is at the beginning of his best period of achievement. Although he does not explain just how this is the result of a woman's sex, the implication is that it is the outcome of the difficulties of her sexual development. To quote him: "It is as though the whole process had been gone through and remained inaccessible to influence for the future; as though in fact the difficult development which leads to femininity had exhausted all the possibilities of the individual."* One might be tempted to believe that because a woman's period of sexual attractiveness is shorter than that of a man she grows old mentally and emotionally earlier. However, here too the cultural factors so dominate the picture that it is hard to see anything else. As long as a woman's sole opportunity for success in life was in making a successful marriage her career was made or lost by the age of thirty. A woman of thirty in the Victorian era and even in some situations today has no

* Sigmund Freud, *New Introductory Lectures on Psychoanalysis* (New York: W. W. Norton, 1933), p. 183.

future. It is well known in psychoanalytic therapy that for successful outcome of treatment an actual opportunity for further development of the person must exist. This consideration would seem to offer an adequate explanation of the greater rigidity of women, if in fact any such greater rigidity can be demonstrated. I believe that there is no dearth of inflexible personalities among men who have reached the height of their development by the age of thirty, whether because of inferior mental equipment, unfortunate early training, or lack of opportunity. Moreover, today there are many examples of women not dependent on their sexual value for security who remain flexible and capable of development. All that may be said with certainty is that woman's lack of opportunity and economic dependence on men can lead to early rigidity and a narrowed outlook on life, as can any situation which curbs spontaneous development in either sex.

What I have said thus far shows that the characteristics of woman which Freud has explained as the result of her biologic vicissitudes beginning with the discovery that she has no penis can be quite as satisfactorily explained in terms of the cultural pressures to which she is subjected. The latter hypothesis must certainly be entertained—if only for economy's sake—before separating the female of man from the realm of general biologic principles and making her something biologically unprecedented.

It is clear that Freud's theories were originally developed about Victorian women. Let me now discuss in contrast the woman of today. The position of woman has changed greatly and if the cultural factors are important she is no longer as sexually inhibited and restricted, her opportunities for self-development are greatly increased, and marriage is no longer the only means of economic security. These facts have undoubtedly influenced the character of women. So much so that a new type of woman is emerging, a woman capable of independence and whose characteristics differ from those described by Freud. However, the present is still a situation of transition. It takes a long time for a cultural change to come about, especially in its psychologic implications for nondependent persons. Something of the Victorian attitude still persists in the psychology of most women. One finds several remnants of it; for example, the notion that it is more womanly for a woman to marry and let a man support her. The majority of women still accept this idea, to be sure not as early in their lives as their grandmothers did. They often have a few years of independence first. For some the alternative of marriage with economic dependence, or independence with or without marriage, presents a serious conflict. Also under the influence of tradition and prejudice many women are convinced that their adequate sexual fulfillment, including children, and an adequate self-development are not to be reconciled. Men have no such tradition and with them the two interests usually reinforce each other. In this, certainly, women still have real grounds for envying men.

In this specific, limited sense Freud's idea that women have envy because they have no penis is symbolically true in this culture. The woman envies the greater freedom of the man, his greater opportunities, and his relative lack of conflict about his fundamental drives. The penis as a symbol of aggression stands for the freedom to be, to force one's way, to get what one wants. These are the characteristics which a woman envies in a man. When this envy is carried to a more pathologic degree the woman thinks of the man as hostile to her and the penis becomes symbolically a weapon which he uses against her. In the pathologic picture called penis envy by Freud the woman wishes to have the destructive qualities she attributes to the man and she wishes to use this destructiveness against him.

There remain to be dealt with the ways in which women have met the problem of feeling inferior to and hating men, or to use the Freudian language, have dealt with their penis envy. Freud outlines three solutions: A woman may accept her feminine role; she may develop neurosis; or her character may develop in the direction of a "masculinity complex." The first of these seemed to him to be the normal solution.

Here again the problem arises as to what is biologic woman and what is cultural woman. Certainly biologically woman can only find her fulfillment as a woman and to the extent to which she denies this she must be frustrated. However, there are other implications in the idea of accepting the feminine role—it may include the acceptance of the whole group of attitudes considered feminine by the culture at the time. In such a sense acceptance of the feminine role may not be an affirmative attitude at all but an expression of submission and resignation. It may mean choosing the path of least resistance with the sacrifice of important parts of the self for security.

The solution of envy of the male by way of neurosis may be considered a solution by evasion, and although many interesting facts could be considered here the influence of the cultural pressures does not differ greatly from that found in the next type of situation.

The solution by way of developing a masculinity complex deserves careful consideration. One significant difference of neurotic character structure from neurosis arises from the fact that the character pattern is in many ways acceptable to the culture. It represents not only a working compromise of the person's conflicting trends, but also takes its pattern directly from the culture. The culture invites masculinity in women. With the passing of the old sheltered life, with the increasing competition with men growing out of the industrial revolution as well as out of women's restlessness, it is not strange that her first steps toward equality would be in the direction of trying to be like men. Having no path of their own to follow women have tended to copy men. Imitating of a person superior to one is by no means unusual. The working man seeking to move up the social and economic scale not only tries to copy the middle-class way of life but may try to adopt the middle-class way of thinking. He may try so hard that he becomes a caricature of the thing he wishes to be, with loss of sight of his real goals in the process.

In the same way women, by aping men, may develop a caricature situation and lose sight of their own interests. Thus, one must consider to what extent it is profitable for a woman to adopt the way of a man. To what extent can she do it without losing sight of her own goals. This leads inevitably to a consideration of what characteristics are biologically male and what have developed secondarily as a result of his way of life. Here, as in the consideration of femininity, the same difficulty in separating biologic and cultural factors is found. Not many years ago a woman's decision to follow a profession—medicine, for example—was considered even by some analysts to be evidence of a masculinity complex. This rose from the belief that all work outside the home, especially if it called for the exercise of leadership, was masculine, and anyone attempting it therefore was trying to be a man.

It is true, practically speaking, that in the business and professional world it often paid to act like a man. Women were entering a domain which had been in the possession of men, in which the so-called masculine traits of decisiveness, daring, and aggression were usually far more effective than the customarily ascribed traits such as gentleness and submissiveness. In adaptation to this new way of life, women could not but tend to change the personality traits acquired from their former cultural setting. The freedom which economic independence brought to women also had its influence in developing characteristics hitherto found only in men. It seems clear, however, that such changes are not in themselves in any fundamental sense in the direction of masculinity. It is not useful to confuse the picture of the independent woman with that of an essentially pathologic character structure, the masculinity complex.[5]

By this, I mean that the culture now favors a woman's developing certain characteristics which have been considered typical of men; but that in addition she may be neurotic and may exploit the cultural situation to protect herself from certain anxieties which have arisen

[5] Notes and References, p. 183.

in part from her difficulties of self-development because she is a woman and in part from other privations and traumata. Obviously, if a woman develops characteristics which indicate that she unconsciously considers herself a man, she is discontent with being a woman. It would be fruitful to inquire what this "being a woman" means to her. I have suggested the possibility of several unpleasant meanings. Being a woman may mean to her being inferior, being restricted, and being in the power of someone. In short, being a woman may mean negation of her feeling of self, a denial of the chance to be an independent person. Refusal to be a woman therefore could mean the opposite, an attempt to assert that one is an independent person. The woman with a masculinity complex shows an exaggerated need for "freedom" and a fear of losing her identity in any intimacy.

It has become clear in the treatment of some related situations that the development of this character pattern is not solely the result of conditioning against being a woman. More basic may be a threat to the personality integrity from an early dependency, a domineering selfish mother, for example, or from the undermining of self-esteem by a destructive mother. In short, many of the forces which make for the development of neurotic mechanisms in general can contribute to this one. These women fear dependency because dependency has been a serious threat to them. Such women are often unable to have any intimate relationship with men; and if they marry, show a hostile revengeful attitude toward the husband. The marriage relationship is sometimes, however, quite successful when circumstances leave them free to work and at least partially support themselves after marriage. Pregnancy is apt to be a special difficulty because of its at least temporary threat to this independence. And they are always afraid of getting into someone's clutches and losing control of the situation.

If the masculinity complex is not developed primarily as a defense against a feeling of biologic lack, if the feeling of cultural inferiority at being a woman is not the sole cause of its development, but on the other hand any difficulty in any important dependency relation can contribute to its formation, why then does it take the particular form of wishing to be or pretending to be a man with associated hatred of men?

Two things in the situation encourage this type of character defense. First, because of the general cultural trend there is secondary gain in such an attitude. It looks like progress and gives the woman the illusion of going along in the direction of the freedom of her time. Second, it offers a means of avoiding the most important intimacy in life, that with a man. This relationship because of its frequent implication of dependency and subordination of the woman's interests especially reactivates all of the dangers of earlier dependencies. The struggle for some form of superiority to men is then an attempt to keep from being destroyed. Men are punished for all that women have been suffering in all sorts of dependency situations.

So it would seem that solution of envy of the male by the development of the masculinity complex does not have a simple origin and that sources not simply relating to sexual comparisons are important in it.

In conclusion, let me say that psychoanalysis thus far has secured extensive acquaintance with the psychology of women in only one type of culture. Facts observed in a particular part of the Western world have been interpreted by Freud as an adequate basis for an understanding of female psychology in general and as evidence for a particular theory about specific biologic factors in the nature of woman. I have pointed out that characteristics and inferiority feelings which Freud considered to be specifically female and biologically determined can be explained as developments arising in and growing out of Western woman's historic situation of underprivilege, restriction of development, insincere attitude toward the sexual nature, and social and economic dependency. The basic nature of woman is still unknown.

Some Effects of the
Derogatory Attitude
toward Female Sexuality

In an earlier paper* I stressed the fact that the actual envy of the penis as such is not as important in the psychology of women as their envy of the position of the male in our society. This position of privilege and alleged superiority is symbolized by the possession of a penis. The owner of this badge of power has special opportunities while those without it have more limited possibilities. I questioned in that paper whether the penis in its own right as a sexual organ was necessarily an object of envy at all.

That there are innate biologic differences between the sexual life of man and woman is so obvious that one must apologize for mentioning it. Yet those who stress this aspect most are too often among the first to claim knowledge of the psychic experiences and feelings of the opposite sex. Thus for many centuries male writers have been busy trying to explain the female. In recent years a few women have attempted to present the inner

* Clara Thompson, " 'Penis Envy' in Women," *Psychiatry*, VI (1943), 123–125.

life of their own sex, but they themselves seem to have had difficulty in freeing their thinking from the male orientation. Psychoanalysts, female as well as male, seem for the most part still to be dominated by Freud's thinking about women.

Freud was a very perceptive thinker but he was a male, and a male quite ready to subscribe to the theory of male superiority prevalent in the culture. This must have definitely hampered his understanding of experiences in a woman's life, especially those specifically associated with her feminine role.

Of course this thinking can be carried to extreme lengths and one can say that no human being can really know what another human being actually experiences about anything. However, the presence of similar organs justifies us in thinking that we can at least approximate an understanding of another person's experiences in many cases. A headache, a cough, a pain in the heart, intestinal cramps, weeping, laughter, joy, a sense of well-being—we assume that all of these feel to other people very similar to what we ourselves experience under those titles.

In the case of sexual experiences, however, one sex has no adequate means of identifying with the experience of the other sex. A woman, for instance, cannot possibly be sure that she knows what the subjective experience of an erection and male orgasm is. Nor can a man identify with the tension and sensations of menstruation, or female genital excitation, or childbirth. Since for many years most of the psychoanalysts were men this may account for the prevalence of some misconceptions about female sexuality. Horney pointed out in 1926 that Freud's theory that little girls believed they had been castrated and that they envied boys their penises is definitely a male orientation to the subject.* In this paper she listed several ideas which little boys have about girls' genitals. These ideas, she shows, are practically identical with the classic psychoanalytic conception of the female. The little boys' ideas are based

* Karen Horney, "Flight from Womanhood," 324–339.

on the assumption that girls also have penises, which results in a shock at the discovery of their absence. A boy, reasoning from his own life experience, assumes this is a mutilation, as a punishment for sexual misdemeanor. This makes more vivid to him any castration threats which have been made to him. He concludes that the girl must feel inferior and envy him because she must have come to the same conclusions about her state. In short, the little boy, incapable of imagining that one could feel complete without a penis, assumes that the little girl must feel deprived. It is doubtless true that her lack of a penis can activate any latent anxiety the boy may have about the security of his own organ, but it does not necessarily follow that the girl feels more insecure because of it.

In "The Economic Problem of Masochism"* Freud assumes that masochism is a part of female sexuality, but he gives as his evidence the fantasies of passive male homosexuals. What a passive male homosexual imagines about the experience of being a woman is not necessarily similar to female sexual experience. In fact, a healthy woman's sexual life is probably not remotely similar to the fantasies and longings of a highly disturbed passive male personality.

Recently I heard to my amazement that a well-known psychiatrist had told a group of students that in the female sexual life there is no orgasm. I can only explain such a statement by assuming that this man could not conceive of orgasm in the absence of ejaculation. If he had speculated that the female orgasm must be a qualitatively different experience from that of the male because of the absence of ejaculation, one could agree that this may well be the case. I think these examples suffice to show that many current ideas about female psychosexual life may be distorted by being seen through male eyes.

In "Sex and Character"† Fromm has pointed out

* Sigmund Freud, "The Economic Problem of Masochism," in *Collected Papers* (5 vols.; New York: Basic Books, Inc., 1959), Vol. II.

† Erich Fromm, "Sex and Character," *Psychiatry*, VI (1943), 21–31.

that the biological differences in the sexual experience may contribute to greater emphasis on one or the other character trends in the two sexes. Thus he notes that for the male it is necessary to be able to perform, while no achievement is required of the female. This, he believes, can have a definite effect on the general character trends. This gives the man a greater need to demonstrate, to produce, to have power, while the woman's need is more in the direction of being accepted, being desirable. Since her satisfaction is dependent on the man's ability to produce, her fear is in being abandoned, being frustrated, while his is fear of failure. Fromm points out that the woman can make herself available at any time and give satisfaction to the man, but the man's possibility of satisfying her is not entirely within his control. He cannot always produce an erection at will.

The effect of basic sexual differences on the character structure is not pertinent to this paper. Fromm's thesis that the ability to perform is important in male sexual life, that it is especially a matter of concern to the male because it is not entirely within his control, and that the female may perform at all times if she so wishes, are points of importance in my thesis. But I should like to develop somewhat different aspects of the situation. Fromm shows that the woman can at any time satisfy the male, and he mentions the male's concern over successfully performing for the female, but he does not at any point discuss how important obtaining satisfaction for themselves is in the total reaction.

In general the male gets at least some physiological satisfaction out of his sexual performance. Some experiences are more pleasurable than others, to be sure, and there are cases of orgasm without pleasure. However, for the very reason that he cannot force himself to perform, he is less likely to find himself in the midst of a totally uncongenial situation.

The female, however, who permits herself to be used when she is not sexually interested or is at most only mildly aroused, frequently finds herself in the midst of an unsatisfactory experience. At most she can have only a vicarious satisfaction in the male's pleasure. I might mention parenthetically here that some male analysts, for example, Ferenczi, are inclined to think that identification with the male in his orgasm constitutes a woman's true sexual fulfillment. This I would question.

One frequently finds resentment in women who have for some reason consented to being used for the male's pleasure. This is in many cases covered by an attitude of resignation. A frequent answer from women when they are asked about marital sexual relations is: "It is all right. He doesn't bother me much." This attitude may hold even when in other respects the husband and wife like each other; that is, such an attitude may exist even when the woman has not been intimidated by threats or violence. She simply assumes that her interests are not an important consideration.

Obviously the sexual act is satisfactory to the woman only when she actively and from choice participates in her own characteristic way. If she considered herself free to choose, she would refuse the male except when she actually did desire to participate.

This being the case, it might be fruitful to examine the situations in which the woman submits with little or no interest. There are, of course, occasions when she genuinely wishes to do this for the man's sake; this does not create a problem. More frequently the cause is a feeling of insecurity in the relationship; this insecurity may arise from external factors—that is, the male concerned may insist on his satisfaction or else! The insecurity may also arise from within because of the woman's own feelings of inadequacy. These feelings may arise simply from the fact that the woman subscribes to the cultural attitude that her needs are not as insistent as the man's; but in addition she may have personal neurotic difficulties.

The question arises: How has it become socially acceptable for a man to insist on his sexual rights whenever he desires? In this because rape is a possibility, and the woman is physically relatively defenseless? This must have had some influence in the course of society's development. However, it has often been proved that even rape is not easy without some cooperation from the woman. The neurotic condition of vaginismus illustrates that in some conditions even unconscious unwillingness on the part of the woman may effectively block male performance. So while the superior physical power of the male may be an important factor in the frequency of passive compliance, there must be other factors. These other factors are not of a biologic nature, for the participation in sexual relations without accompanying excitement is most obviously possible in human females, although not definitely impossible in other animals.

One must look to cultural attitudes for the answer. There are two general concepts which are significant here, and to which both men and women subscribe in our culture. One is that the female sexual drive is not as pressing or important as the male. Therefore there is less need to be concerned in satisfying it or considering it. The other is the analytically much-discussed thesis that the female sex organs are considered inferior to those of the male.

In recent years there has been a definite tendency to move away from the first idea as far as actual sexual performance is concerned. With the increasing tendency to be more open in observing facts about sex, women in many groups have become able not only to admit to themselves but also to men that their sexual needs are important. However, this is still not true of all groups. Moreover, at almost the same time another important aspect of woman's sexual life has diminished in importance; that is, the bearing of children. Woman's specific type of creativeness is no longer highly desired in many situations. This is an important subject in itself and will not be discussed here.

As we know, during the Victorian era a woman's sexual needs were supposed to be practically nonexistent. A woman was expected to be able to control her sexual desires at all times. Thus an extramarital pregnancy was allegedly entirely due to the woman's weakness or depravity. The man's participation in such an extramarital relationship was looked upon with more tolerance, and there was little or no social disgrace attached to him. The double standard of sexual morality also implied an assumption that woman's sexual drive was not as insistent as the male's.

The fact that evidence of erotic excitement could be concealed much better by a woman than by a man made the development of such thinking possible. Since she was not supposed to be erotic and since the man must have his satisfaction, a pattern was developed in which the dutiful wife offered herself to her husband without actively participating in the act herself. I am sure many women were sufficiently normal to find non-participation difficult, and doubtless many men did not subscribe to the feeling that they should be horrified at any evidence of passion in their wives. Nevertheless, as recently as twenty years ago a woman, who consulted me about her marital difficulties, reported that her husband felt disgust, it seemed, whenever she responded sexually to him. She tried to conceal her sexual responses, including orgasm, from him, then would lie awake the rest of the night in misery and rage. Since I saw this woman only twice, I am not in a position to say how much this situation contributed to her suicide about a year later. Undoubtedly there were many other difficulties in her relation to her husband, of which the sexual may have been only one expression. Certainly this extreme denial of sexual interest is seldom required of women today, but an attenuated form still remains, especially in marriage. Here it is found not only in frigid women who, realizing their inadequacy as mates, make amends as best they can by a nonparticipating offering of themselves. But one also finds the attitude even in women with adequate sexual responsiveness in many situations. They have accepted the idea that the male's needs are greater than their own and that therefore his wishes and needs are paramount.

So the feeling that woman's sexual life is not as important or insistent as the male's may produce two unfortunate situations. It may inhibit the woman's natural expression of desire for fear of appearing un-womanly, or it may lead her to feel she must be ready to accommodate on all occasions—that is, she has no rights of her own. Both extremes mean an interference with her natural self-expression and spontaneity with resulting resentment and discontent.

Moreover, since the male has often been indoctrinated with the idea that woman's sexual life is not important, he may not exert himself much to make her interested. He fails to see the importance of the art of love.

When an important aspect of a person's life becomes undervalued, this has a negative effect on the self-esteem. What a woman actually has to offer in sexual responsiveness becomes undervalued, and this in turn affects her own evaluation of herself as a person.

The second way in which our culture has minimized woman's sexual assets is in the derogation of her genitals. This in classic terminology is connected with the idea of penis envy. I wish to approach the problem differently. As I said earlier, the idea of penis envy is a male concept. It is the male who experiences the penis as a valuable organ and he assumes that women also must feel that way about it. But a woman cannot really imagine the sexual pleasure of the penis—she can only appreciate the social advantages its possessor has.* What a woman needs rather is a feeling of the importance of her own organs. I believe that much more important than penis envy in the psychology of woman in her reaction to the undervaluation of her own organs. I think we can concede that the acceptance of one's body and all its functions is a basic need in the establishment of self-respect and self-esteem.

The short, plump brunette may feel that she would be more acceptable if she were a tall, thin blond—in other words, if she were somebody else. The solution of her problem lies not in becoming a blond but in finding out why she is not accepting what she is. The history will show either that some significant person in her early life preferred a tall blond or that being a brunette

---

* I do not wish to leave the impression that there is never a woman who thinks she desires to possess the male genital as such, but I believe such women are found relatively rarely.

has become associated with other unacceptable characteristics. Thus in one case in which this envy of the blond type was present, being brunette meant being sexy, and being sexy was frowned upon.

Sex in general has come under the disapproval of two kinds of thinking in our culture. The puritan ideal is denial of body pleasure, and this makes sexual needs something of which to be ashamed. Traces of this attitude still remain today in the feelings of both sexes.

We also have another attitude which derogates sexuality, especially female sexuality. We are people with great emphasis on cleanliness. In many people's minds the genital organs are classed with the organs of excretion and thus become associated with the idea of being unclean. With the male some of the curse is removed because he gets rid of the objectionable product. The female, however, receives it, and when her attitude is strongly influenced by the dirty excretion concept, this increases her feeling of unacceptability. Moreover, the men who feel the sexual product is unclean reinforce the woman's feeling that her genitals are unclean.

The child's unrestrained pleasure in his body and its products begins to be curbed at an early age. This is such a fundamental part of our basic training that most of us would have difficulty imagining the effect on our psychic and emotional life of a more permissive attitude. What has happened is that this training has created a kind of moral attitude toward our body products. Sphincter morality, as Ferenczi has called it, extends to more than the control of urine and feces. To some extent genital products come also under the idea of sphincter morality. Obviously this especially has an influence on attitudes toward the female genitals where no sphincter control is possible. My attention was first called to this by a paper written in German by Bertram Lewin twenty years ago.* In this paper he presented, among other things, clinical data in which the menses were compared to an unwanted loss of feces and urine

* Bertram Lewin, "Kotschmieren, Menses und weibliches Über-Ich," *Internationale Zeitschrift fuer Psychoanalysis*, XVI (1930), 43–56.

due to lack of sphincter control. In one case which he reported the woman had become very proficient at contracting the vaginal muscles so that she attained some semblance of control of the quantity of menstrual flow. Although in my own practice I have never encountered a patient who actually tried to produce a sphincter, I have frequent evidence that the inability not only to control menstruation but all secretions of the female genitals has contributed to a feeling of unacceptability and dirtiness. One patient on being presented by her mother with a perineal napkin on the occasion of her first menses refused to use it. To her it meant a baby's diaper, and she felt completely humiliated. Obviously she presently felt even more humiliated because of the inevitable consequences of her refusal.

Also because of the culture's overevaluation of cleanliness another attribute of the female genital can be a source of distress, that is, the fact that it has an odor. Thus one of the chief means by which the female attracts the male among animals has been labeled unpleasant, to many even disgusting. For example, a female patient whose profession requires her appearing before audiences has been greatly handicapped for many years by a feeling of being "stinking" which is greatly augmented whenever she is in a position to have her body observed. Thus she can talk over the radio but not before an audience. Another patient felt for years that she could never marry because she would not be able to keep her body clean at every moment in the presence of her husband. Whenever she had a date with a man she prepared for it by a very vigorous cleansing of the genitals, especially trying to make them dry. When she finally had sexual relations she was surprised and greatly helped in her estimation of her body by discovering that this highly prized dryness was just the opposite of what was pleasing to the man.

In two cases the feeling of genital unacceptability had been a factor in promiscuity. In each case an experience with a man who kissed her genitals in an obviously accepting way was the final step in bringing about a complete transformation of feeling. In both cases all need to be promiscuous disappeared, and each of the women felt loved for the first time.

I am obviously oversimplifying these cases in order to make my point clear. I do not wish to leave the impression that the feeling of dirtiness connected with the genitals was the sole cause of a feeling of unacceptability in these patients. There was in each case a feeling from early childhood of not being acceptable, produced by specific attitudes in the parents. The feeling of unacceptability became focused on the genitals eventually for different reasons in each case. For example, in three cases the woman had risen above the lowly social position of her parents and with each of these three women the feeling of having dirty genitals became symbolic of her lowly origin of which she was ashamed. The parents had not placed such an emphasis on baths as they found to be the case in the new social milieu. Therefore any evidence of body secretion or odor betrayed them, and this made sex itself evidence of lower-class origin. On the other hand, two other patients suffered from their own mothers' overemphasis on body cleanliness. In each of these two cases the mother was cold and puritanical as well as overclean, and the patient felt humiliated because she had a more healthy sexual drive which she felt was proclaimed to the world by her body's odors and secretions.[6]

From these observations I hope I have emphasized the fact that the problem of a woman's sexual life is in accepting her own sexuality in its own right.

[6] Notes and References, p. 183.

Working Women

People develop in the directions in which they can go. In an expanding or rapidly changing society, the potential possibilities are many. In a more fixed society, the choices are more limited. At the same time, in the fixed society, the conflict is less because one does not have to choose and discard this for that. Women in the American culture today have wider choices than before, at the same time that the life previously traditionally expected of them has become, in many ways, more unsatisfactory since the beginning of the twentieth century. Middle-class and professional women especially are unhappy confining themselves exclusively to home activity. They feel left behind with their innate capacities going to waste. Even during the years when their children are small and their time is fully occupied, many of them have a feeling of futility about what they are doing. Even more the alert married woman, whose time is no longer fully occupied with small children, feels apologetic and unimportant. On the other hand, very few women are satisfied with the opposite choice of being career women without marriage. They, also, usually feel apologetic and failures, and one finds each type envying the other.

The bachelor woman is still not as socially and economically secure as the bachelor man. Economically, she is seldom as well paid, and she is discarded sooner than the man as she grows older. Socially, she has fewer opportunities for stimulating companionship. She is much less welcome at a dinner party than an unattached male. The popular belief is that stag parties are fun, while hen parties are boring. The validity of these assumptions can be questioned, but they give us a picture of the attitudes women must face. The unmarried career woman, therefore, has a feeling of inferiority, as well as lack of fulfillment. The inferiority feeling is due, in part, to her not having entirely discarded old standards, i.e., a feeling of humiliation about failing to marry. A restless loneliness is one of the most frequent problems leading unmarried career women to seek psychoanalytic help.

Even when she finds the work she is doing satisfying, it does not adequately compensate for human intimacy and children. Many women have partially solved the problem by having affairs or by establishing a homosexual ménage. Affairs are precarious, because they give no security for companionship in old age. Try as they will, act as emancipated as possible, most women who have not married have a feeling of failure. On deeper probing one finds doubts of themselves as women. A great number of affairs seldom reassures a woman that she is accepted or loved. She may talk very loudly about her independence, but when she begins to feel indications that the current man is about to depart, she is very disturbed and feels [that she is] a failure. She does not often succeed in taking sexual experiences casually. She usually has a tendency to want to bind *the man*. About this matter, married women often have similar difficulties because of present-day ease of divorce. Men, on the other hand, are supposed to be less concerned about permanency. I say "supposed" because I wonder how extensively the fantasy life of the two sexes on this matter has been compared. Because it has been easier for the man to put his fantasy into action on this point, have we perhaps erroneously assumed he has more desire to do so?

However, there are one or two points about a woman's desire for permanency which should be considered. First, has the ever-present possibility of pregnancy built a deep biologic need for continuity into woman's nature? Many writers believe that this is the case, that the woman feels she has received a very special gift from the man which ties her to him, while a man conceivably thinks of his semen more as something discarded and having no further interest for him.

Whether this attitude holds true basically for human nature in general cannot be demonstrated. Certainly, in matriarchies, women have *seemed* not to need this continuity. Second, we know that in our society other factors contribute to it. Our women have not the assurance of a long-established tradition of independence. Many have no training which would make it possible to live comfortably on what they could earn. Even when they are highly trained, most of them feel relatively helpless and weak in the competitive world, and they do, in fact, have a harder time than men. So, for the great majority of women still, there is no financial security comparable to that of marriage. Also, the divorced woman has a little harder time socially than the divorced man. She, again, becomes the extra woman, while his status may continue the same or actually be improved. In short, much of a woman's craving for permanency is the result of tradition and her economic situation. The matriarchal woman does not seem to have needed to be firmly attached to a particular male. If the society in which a woman lives permits her, a woman is able to fend for herself and her young. . . . Our present industrial culture does not favor it.

We must consider at least one more important factor influencing woman's development in our society. Today, she is in conflict as to what and who she is. She is educated in two directions at the same time. On the one hand, she receives the same education in the competitive ways of our society as a man does. She is indoctrinated with the idea of success, being on top, getting the highest salary or the greatest publicity. On the other hand, she expects to marry and have children. In this job she gets no fixed salary, and the amount of money she receives is not dependent on her competence. Having a large family is usually a calamity, and the type of work she does in the home leaves her with little tangible evidence of achievement. Meals disappear, dishwashing, laundry, and house cleaning must be perpetually repeated. She feels apologetic and unproductive for she is still influenced by her education in competitiveness. Certainly, today, fewer women marry simply to have "Mrs." on their gravestones, but neither is the healthy woman willing, altogether, to renounce motherhood for a career.

It is in the area of the need to find some way of being a mother and a professional woman that the practical difficulties arise. Obviously, it is at the point where practical difficulties seem almost insuperable that many neurotic solutions are made. So the aggressive woman tries to play down her mother role and assert her right to be just like a man. Or she accepts the prescribed feminine role and expresses her resentment in her relationship to husband and children. The masochistic type feels guilty because of her ambitions and may become oversolicitous of her children. The woman who feels rejected may take advantage of today's freedom by having many men, etc.

. . . Any attempt to change a cultural pattern produces conflict in the people involved. Those who have had the advantage previously and have little or nothing to gain from the change, i.e., in this case, men, furnish a strong resistance to the change. The result may be increasing the woman's inferiority feelings or her sense of guilt at wanting to be different. Women of the twentieth century have tried to redefine their position in society, but, as yet, no adequate provision for motherhood and other creative work has been made except in individual cases. Human society is always changing in some way or other. At the present time, the status of women seems to be in an especially fluid state. Under the circumstances, even the healthy woman finds conflicts, and there will be no rest until a relatively stable compromise is reached.

The group of women who marry and in addition

engage in a business or professional life are perhaps the most typical product of our present culture. The solution of the conflicts rising out of their situation should be especially helpful in creating the woman of the future. They encounter two types of problems: those connected with their relationship to their husbands, and those connected with the problem of children and a career.

Let us consider first the problem with husbands. There is the ideal situation in which both husband and wife are interested in each other's achievement without being competitive in any way. It is more likely to work when the two are engaged in different types of occupation, or at least in slightly different fields.

Unfortunately, the situation frequently is more disturbed. The husband's resentment and competitive attitude may crush the wife's initiative. He feels that his virility is threatened, that people will think he cannot support her, or he fears that he will lose his power over her, and so forth. In such situations, if the marriage continues, the wife must give up her work.

Sometimes the opposite is the case and the wife proves to be the better breadwinner. Because this is culturally a revolutionary situation it can make a great many difficulties and both husband and wife need inner security in order to accept the situation. . . . However, I know of two marriages where the woman's money-making capacity was accepted by the husband and he did a good share of the housework, without resentment and as a matter of course.

In short, one must say it is the unusual husband and wife who can accept with equanimity a situation in which the woman is the more successful one in terms of money or prestige. The whole cultural attitude is against the acceptance of this. It has been known for centuries that many women solve the problem by playing stupid. Never let your husband know that you know more about anything than he does unless it happens to be cooking or something about which he has no interest. Of course there are women who find pleasure in

humiliating their men, but these are definitely pathologic types. I believe many women would be happy today
to be psychologically free to accept, without malice
toward their husbands, the importance of their own
position. If she could but recognize, for instance, that
the disgrace of earning more money than her husband
is based on the old patriarchal idea that he ought to
own her, each of them would certainly feel less conflict
about it. She might in fact be quite happy. But this
attitude, I'm afraid, belongs to the future. It is a goal
for which couples may strive, but very few have actually achieved it to date.

Even more difficult of solution is the problem of
having children and at the same time successfully competing in a man's world. The trouble with childbearing
and rearing children is that it is only temporarily a
full-time job. In our present economy large families are
no longer desirable. A woman has a full-time job as a
mother only for a few years. After that, if she has lost
touch with her former interests, her life can be pretty
sterile. This is the problem for which some practical
solution is needed. If women are to stay in business an
adjustment to this problem must be found. And if
women are not to stay in business and professions then
something else will have to be found for them to do. I
do not believe the large number of women who are
today restless and without goals will be content to
remain this way indefinitely. Let us remember that
many of these people were financially independent before marriage and know what it is to do work which
gives them satisfaction.

Many women of course solve the problem by choosing between children and a profession. Each woman
has her own reasons for the choice. It is fortunate when
the choice has found unconscious emotional roots, that
is, when women really choose what the deepest part of
their natures wants. If a woman's life experience has
brought her to the point of not really wanting to have
children it is sad for everyone if she feels constrained to
have them. She will not be happy and their lives will be

disturbed by it. Nevertheless, it still happens that women with very little flair for motherhood do every now and then sell themselves the idea that the complete woman must have children.

If it were merely a question of carrying on *some* work during the years when children need much attention, many women would be able to make the adjustment. But our economic system is such that in many types of work a woman cannot slow down her work without losing out altogether. So she must either continue at her former pace and leave much of the care of her children to others or she must run the risk of getting out of touch with her work or profession. In the latter case she may find it very hard to return later when she has the leisure.

Let us consider a little the woman who tries to do both. I have no experience with women with whom the two drives had equal value. One always seems to be a little more weighted with importance than the other. The less important one then suffers from neglect. This is the temporarily insoluble problem of many professional women today. How to keep both without damaging one or the other. I do not believe Dr. Farnham's solution of returning to the home can be the answer. The home as it was one hundred years ago no longer exists nor can it be re-created in the present society. When women left the home for business and the professions they adopted as their guide the standards of men. This was a part of the idea of equality, and also there was no other way to do it. In this acceptance of the male standard I believe they somehow lost touch with the unique value of being women. By comparing themselves with men they placed themselves in unequal competition with men. They forgot that women are neither superior nor inferior to men—but different. Women have not yet found their new place in the social order. As long as they try to compete with men on equal terms they are at a disadvantage because they are not men. They cannot return to their old position because it no longer exists. It is certain that they will never be happy trying to be men. Such a procedure would leave out of consideration a woman's real contribution. So she is doomed to feeling inferior as long as she believes she must act just like a man. She cannot find the importance of her own place as long as she accepts for herself the masculine standard of achievement.

Women must learn to find importance and dignity in their own functions. They must struggle against leading empty and unproductive lives without feeling they must necessarily become a part of the competitive system of our culture, a system created by males in which males have a distinct advantage.

How does this apply practically? It is very difficult. So far there is very little general movement in the direction of finding a solution. Individual women have found ways of being good mothers and at the same time leading productive lives satisfactory to themselves. The social order is already making some concessions to the biologic function of women. In some situations there are pregnancy leaves and the possibility of returning to work later. Maybe these leaves should be longer, with more consideration of the importance of a mother's care in early childhood. The future of the human race in a way depends on women thinking more about their own special problem and less about being just like men.

This seems to be a keynote to the problem. Are women ready to recognize that they have a unique contribution to make? As long as they must try to be men they will miss the goal of their own lives. A rose cannot become a potato, and obviously there is no reason why the rose should try. When women tried to become free they accepted as their blueprint the masculine pattern. There was no other example. Now they should try to find their own pattern.

In the search for their own pattern perhaps it would help to remember that the competitive race for success does not enrich the lives of the people caught in it. Moreover it is a race in which women are at a distinct disadvantage because of their biologic function. They might well become leaders in bringing about a change in attitude about competition. If they themselves can find a way of leading fruitful lives without becoming involved in the competitive system they will have started a change in the attitude of the culture itself.

Middle Age

In important ways, the meaning of each stage of life is dependent on what happened in the preceding stages. During the years before middle age the average person is not quite so aware of this. He has the feeling, for instance, "Even if my childhood wasn't happy this is all going to be changed now by a happy marriage—or I'll have the satisfaction of making a better life for my children." Or he doesn't like his job—he can look for another one. It may be that none of these things happens, but at least he hopes. He feels himself still young, strong, and capable of conquering. But the term middle age has a frightening sound for most people. Somehow it means you are passing the peak—your powers are beginning to wane—you are not as robust—you cannot start new things now. Especially for women there also lurks some vague nightmare called the change of life which in popular thinking is accompanied by terrible somatic difficulties and even the specter of insanity. You will argue that these superstitions cannot be wholly false. A fear that is so widespread must have some basis in observable fact.

Let us investigate these negative aspects and attempt to place them in their true perspective and then consider the too-little-publicized positive satisfactions of middle age.

When we think of middle life, we think roughly of a period somewhere between the ages of forty and sixty years. But this was not always so, nor is it necessarily true of many people today. In the early 1900's, Freud was of the opinion that in the case of women not many changes could be made in their lives after thirty. He believed that somehow the difficult process of becoming a woman had so exhausted her adaptive powers that by the time she was thirty she was already fixed and rigid in her personality—one could say already past middle age in adaptability. Freud has usually been an accurate observer of facts but often he saw things as more unalterable, more biologically determined than they really are. Subsequent development of our way of life has certainly greatly altered this pessimistic appraisal of women. In 1900, a woman of thirty in middle-class European society usually found her life course rigidly determined. If she had not married by then she was doomed to spinsterhood—and that was a very limiting and bleak outlook. If she had married, she was inescapably committed. If her marriage was unhappy, there was no way of changing this, short of the death of her husband. Few women had been educated to the point of having other sources of interest or satisfaction. And, of course, as a psychotherapist, Freud was not consulted by the happily married woman. (I assume there were some in 1900.) Hence, the possibility of a woman's enlarging or enriching her life much after the age of thirty seemed indeed small at that time.

* * *

Anything which tends to limit a person's free development tends to make him rigid and prematurely old. A man caught in an uninteresting, routine job without the opportunity for advancement will also become rigid and old before his time, unless he has other compensations, such as a happy marriage or a lively interest in something other than his work. In other words, a person tends to remain young if he has a future, that is, if he can continue to grow and develop.

One of the forces which tends to prevent this is lack of opportunity. This lack of opportunity may be the result of inadequate educational advantages due to poverty, racial discrimination, or other restrictions of the particular social order under which one lives. Another force leading to early old age is a limitation within the personality itself, such as low intelligence or crippling neurosis.

If we take these factors into consideration, it is apparent that the time of middle age is partly dependent on social and personality forces and is not a definite chronologic period. Thus one may be fixed and rigid at the age of twenty, or one finds people such as Titian, Einstein, or Goethe still creative and productive at the age of seventy and even eighty. Although exceptions in both directions exist, for practical purposes in this discussion, we will stick to the average, i.e., what happens to most people between forty and sixty.

What are the hazards of middle age? We begin to die from the moment of birth. That is, throughout life, from time to time, certain organs reach the height of their function and begin to deteriorate. For example, the thymus gland is one of the organs which begin to diminish at birth and in normal people has become rudimentary by the age of five. In the meantime, other organs are developing and for many years, physically, there is more growth in the body than deterioration. Then comes a period of relative equilibrium—this is middle age, a kind of pause in life before our physical strength starts downhill, that is, when the rate of deterioration is faster than the rate of growth. However, not even in this physical sphere do all people arrive at this middle stage at the same time. We encounter people with snow-white hair in the twenties, and we find people in the seventies with hardly a gray hair. I do not wish to give the impression that white hair is necessarily a sign of general aging of the body, but simply to illustrate the wide range of aging of various parts. Much more important than hair in affecting the whole personality are the variations in aging of the arteries and other vital organs.

In the physical sphere, middle age is best known to people in general as the time of the change of life in women. Sometime during middle age women come to the end of their capacity for reproduction. This is marked by the cessation of menstruation and is accompanied by a general readjusting of the endocrine balance in the body. The endocrines are organs secreting various hormones which when in balance cooperate with each other in aiding the functioning of the body. When one is changed, as, for example, when the thyroid gland becomes underactive, this affects the functioning of other endocrine glands. The ovaries, for instance, are then disturbed in their functioning and a woman with deficient thyroid may be unable to become pregnant, although there is nothing basically wrong with her ovaries.

In the same way, at the menopause, the ovaries gradually cease to function. With the diminishing of ovarian function the other endocrines are temporarily thrown out of balance, and this produces some of the physical discomforts of this period. The most well known of these are the so-called hot flashes that overtake a woman unexpectedly from time to time. Today, however, these physical discomforts can be markedly diminished, and in some cases entirely overcome, by supplying the missing hormones and withdrawing them more gradually than nature does. Women no longer need anticipate with dread the physical discomforts of the change of life. Many women experience almost no unpleasant symptoms and can mark the time of the menopause only by the cessation of menstruation.

But the question which concerns us here is why do women tend more easily to get upset at this time. Various factors play a part. One cannot deny that the physical instability just described contributes somewhat. When you never know when you are going to be too hot or too cold, when menstruation arrives at unpredictable moments or just as annoyingly fails to appear so that you never know whether you are pregnant or not, there is likely to be an increased feeling of uncertainty and this makes for increased irritability.

One gets angry more easily, one weeps more easily. But if life in general is happy these disturbances are usually of a minor nature.

The serious emotional upsets of the middle years are due, not primarily to physical conditions per se, but to the awareness more or less consciously of the unlived life. The physical change brings a woman sharply up against the fact that she is beginning to age. She may have been drifting along from year to year in a frustrated, discontented, unproductive life, somehow continuing to hope that the future will be better. Suddenly, with the menopause, she realizes with dismay that it is too late now. The spinster, who has waited through the years for the right man to come along, is now faced with the fact that he has not come and probably will not. This type of woman is not so frequent today as she was formerly, but one still occasionally sees her in the psychiatrist's office.

For example, there is the case of an unmarried schoolteacher living in a private girls' school. For many years, she was happy in this adolescent atmosphere, living emotionally herself at the adolescent level. The beginning of the menopause suddenly threw her into a panic. She had always expected some day to get around to marrying—now she must hurry up to find the man; but this meant getting out of this girls' school. But, when she got out, she found, of course, that she was not prepared to find a man. She sank into a paranoid psychosis, in which she believed that all young men who came near her were trying to seduce her. The butcher was putting powder in her food designed to rouse her sexually. The mail carrier had his tricks. She moved from grocer to grocer, and job to job, trying to escape these persecutors. She even took a trip to Europe, but the persecutors were there. Although this woman was in torment, nevertheless in a distorted way she was denying that it was too late to find love. Witness—all the men in the world are after her. Of course, not every disappointed spinster becomes as disturbed as this.

Another who suddenly thinks it is too late is the

unhappily married woman who has remained with her husband for the sake of her children, or because she is afraid to venture on her own. If she has remained in an unhappy situation because of her children she usually thinks: "When my children are old enough I will leave him," but when the time comes she is unable to conceive of an independent life, for now she doubts her sexual charm, or she fears no men are available.

There is another type of woman for whom middle age is a hazard, and that is the woman who has depended a great deal for self-esteem on her ability to attract male admirers. She may have been very beautiful or she may have had unusual charm, but she lacks a firm foundation within herself. At heart she does not believe in herself. For her middle age brings panic as she begins to realize that her way of adjustment is coming to an end. These women in their forties often start a hectic pursuit of men. They engage in frantic efforts to appear young. They indeed are in the roaring forties.

Even the happily married woman may have a few qualms about her fears of loss of sexual attractiveness. And one frequently gets inquiries such as "Will I still be capable of sexual desire?"! About the latter there is an unequivocal yes. If you have enjoyed your sexual life up until the menopause, you will continue to enjoy it in many instances even into old age. In my practice I have been consulted by women over seventy because they were still "bothered by" (to use the expression of one) sexual feelings. They feared that they were somehow depraved. For these few who consult psychiatrists, there must be thousands who continue to enjoy their sexual life after seventy without conflict. At any rate, one does not have to fear the loss of sexual interest after the menopause.

In short, emotionally the menopause poses the greatest threat to two types of women: those who have postponed living until too late and those who have managed to maintain a feeling of importance and value only through the adulation of men. These are the people who have breakdowns and are consumed with self-reproaches about their misspent lives.

Many of these women live through this experience and come out successfully to find new interests. This is especially true if they have had psychiatric help, but some find their way back to an interest in life by themselves. Not infrequently they find an outlet in some form of cause which they adopt as a kind of religion or a genuine interest. But women are not the only ones who find middle life a frightening hazard. To be sure, men do not have an actual organic change of life. As you know, men keep the power of procreation until well into old age. Healthy men as well as healthy women also keep the power of sexual enjoyment until old age. But for men the fulfillment of this latter satisfaction is easier to obtain in middle age, and even in the sixties, than it is for women.

Furthermore, especially with women, but also to some extent with men, another situation usually occurring at middle age adds a hazard to the time. With the average marriage, children have reached adolescence by the time their parents are forty-five. They are beginning to leave home, to manage their lives more and more on their own. A hundred years ago, this was not so true. In the large families of the early pioneering days, a woman continued to bear children throughout her reproductive life. Therefore, she might still be concerned with raising a two- or three-year-old at forty-five. But today, in families of two or three children, most of them are breaking away when their parents are in the forties. This throws the parents back on their own inner resources. The woman sees her job which had required so much of her energies up until now disappearing. Presently two people married for many years and engaged in a joint enterprise find themselves alone together, the woman practically without employment and feeling insecure because of her diminishing sexual charm. The way this situation works out depends again on the nature of the intimacy of these two people up to this point. Have there been many interests in common, mutual respect? Does the woman have a sympathetic interest in her husband's business, or has she the initiative to seek new work for herself? Can he understand her problem without being threatened? If there was no deep feeling of mutual liking and respect earlier in the marriage, the marriage may break up by the husband going elsewhere. The woman is likely to cling frantically to her husband, to become more possessive and jealous, or try to keep his attention and control him by obscure physical complaints. These signs of panic on her part often only increase the gulf between the two, although sometimes it looks as if they have become more devoted because she has managed to make her husband feel guilty for his impulses toward freedom. But in spite of all these hazards of middle age, a surprising number of people go through it very well.

Although the onset of middle age is a period of crisis, in that a new way of life is beginning, it does not have to be a tragic period characterized by a frantic effort to hold on to youth. Middle age definitely has its rewards, and the door is not closed to growth and development for those who have not been so successful earlier, if they will turn toward the satisfactions available in middle life and not try to become adolescents again.

First let us consider the happiest experience possible in middle life. That is the experience of having arrived. The early struggles in making a place for oneself in the business or professional world are ended. Uncertainties are past. Years of devotion and experience have gone into building a secure foundation in business or home, and at last the results are apparent. You can see with satisfaction your own worth! A man of my acquaintance started in a business as office boy at the age of fourteen. At sixty, he became president of the company. Many years of struggle and hard work lay between these two points. Unfortunately, such a success story seldom occurs today. He belonged to the generation before mine, but advancement in business still occurs and such men find themselves at fifty or sixty securely placed and recognized as experts in their fields.

The professional man or woman has the greatest opportunity to have the experience of recognized success. The successful medical man or lawyer, for instance, usually has more demands on his time than he can give by the time he is forty-five. Freed from anxieties about making a living he is able to devote himself to the more interesting aspects of his work. He can leave the drudgery to younger people. But you will say these are special cases; these are the ones who in the beginning either had special endowment or unusual opportunity, and that is true. Outstanding success comes to relatively few of the millions of Americans, but the satisfaction of having lived well and productively can be experienced for many other less spectacular achievements. For example, the man and woman who brought up a healthy family can look on with joy at their starting out in life. The man who has worked hard and finally is able to buy the home he always wanted can also have the feeling of having arrived. The woman who sees her first grandchild, the offspring of the happy marriage of her son or daughter, can also enjoy the feeling of achievement. Thus middle age can bring the fulfillment of earlier promise.

For the emotionally healthy person the feeling of having arrived is not a signal to stop growing. Many go right on growing in the same direction, e.g., the medical man continues to keep up with the advances in his field and is in a better position to contribute to them because of his long experience. The man who buys a house may become interested in beautifying it or developing his garden. But for many, continued growth in middle life may mean finding new interests, and this is especially true of most women. The grandmother cannot indefinitely find her chief joy in her grandchildren. Their actual lives in this generation usually touch her life infrequently. The woman of middle life who has been chiefly a mother and homemaker must find new interests that are personally satisfying if she is to continue to grow. Many women have a kind of rebirth after menopause. Their general health is better. Freed from concern about possible pregnancy their sex lives often become more spontaneous and satisfying. Although there is no longer the fiery passion of youth, sex becomes expressive of a tried and trusted companionship and intimacy often more satisfactory in its total meaning than earlier experiences. Especially fortunate is the woman who earlier prepared herself for the years when she would have more time. For example, there is a woman who was a musician of modest talent before her marriage. The responsibilities of marriage, children, and finally two years of nursing a dying husband led to neglect of her musical interests; but at fifty-five she turned back to it again. She became a professional accompanist in a small way and thus brought herself again into contact with a whole world of new interests which actually made her grow younger. Another woman had some experience in administrative work before marriage. She gave this up because of her husband's objection and there followed a childless marriage in which she was restless and increasingly hypochondriacal. She went from doctor to doctor and, as the menopause approached, it looked as if she could not escape a breakdown. But with some psychoanalytic help, she got the happy idea of using her earlier administrative experience in her husband's business. He was still rather old-fashioned about a wife's working, but he came to see that it was important for her psychic health and gave her the chance. From then on until his death and the sale of the business, this woman enjoyed better mental health than she had known since her marriage. She grew to love her husband more fully. Her middle age and old age proved to be productive periods of growth. I might say (although this is outside of middle age) that since her husband's death, she has found another job in which she is greatly interested, although she is now over seventy.

This last case brings us to our third consideration. We have seen that the fulfilled early life generally leads to a productive middle age, that serious frustration and discontent in the early years can lead to mental illness and despair in the middle years. Our last consideration is: Do difficulty and unhappiness earlier have to lead to more unhappiness later? The case I have just mentioned is an example of triumphing over the unhappy past. Another example is a woman who consulted me many years ago. She was about fifty at the time, and she was married to a mean, parsimonious, hypocritically religious man whose temper had always terrified her. She had four children, the youngest of whom was then thirteen. All of the children had serious emotional difficulties—in fact, from her description the youngest seemed well on the way to schizophrenia. Needless to say, the woman was an excellent example of the menopausal type of panic one sees when the awareness of an unlived life dawns on a person. However, there was a quality of vitality about this woman that made me feel something could be done for her. She went far beyond what I had dreamed of for her. She had a native knack of being able to help people feel out their difficulties, but she had no education beyond high school and no type of training. Soon after her few talks with me—this was not an analysis—she left her husband, although he made it as difficult as possible for her, proceeded to put herself through college, taking a few courses a year while she supported herself doing this and that. Today she is a teacher and counselor in a sanitarium for crippled children, and has a regular column in her local newspaper on parent-child problems. I think she will get her degree in another year. It is true that her past life has left her with personality difficulties, but she has had a rebirth and she has more possibilities for growth and development than ever before. Also her two younger children have shown improvement with her change.

There is also the woman of fifty, who hopes, by dyeing her hair, having her face lifted, and wearing youthful clothes, to have the sexual charm and allure of a woman of thirty. She is doomed to failure in her attempts at salvaging her misspent life. People sometimes come to analysis for miracles. One must first face and come to terms with the fact that one can never make up for the lost years. One can only hope to live from now on. And for that, middle age is not too late to begin—to begin with the pleasures and satisfactions possible in middle life.

A Brief Biography

Clara Mabel Thompson was born on October 3, 1893, in Providence, Rhode Island, and grew up in relatively comfortable circumstances in a large house, built for her parents at the time of their marriage, on the outskirts of the city.

Her upbringing, in the bosom of an extended family that included grandparents both maternal and paternal, a brother nine years her junior, and various aunts and uncles, would have been considered "normal" for her time and class, and was indeed an archetype of Americana: whatever the actual American norm, the popular image of such a "typical" American family still lingers, and its attitudes and values were strongly reflected in Clara Thompson both as a girl and as a mature adult.

Her secondary schooling, 1908–1912, was obtained at the Classical High School in Providence; her choice of a career was already determined at this time. She announced at a meeting of the Baptist Christian Endeavor that she intended to become a medical missionary, and did not swerve from that declared purpose until her medical training was virtually complete.

In September, 1912, she entered the Women's College of Brown University in Providence to begin her premedical studies; one of her college summers was spent working with mental patients at the Danvers

(Mass.) State Hospital. But it was not until after she had begun actual medical training at Johns Hopkins, entering in 1916, that she decided to specialize in psychiatry. Among the influences leading to the decision was that of Lucille Dooley, who held a doctorate of psychology from Clark University. An invitation from the older woman led her to spend a summer working at St. Elizabeth's Hospital in Washington, D.C., where she had the good fortune to come in contact with William Alanson White, then superintendent of the hospital.

After graduation in 1920, Clara Thompson spent a year at Johns Hopkins as a psychiatric intern, then took a rotating internship at the New York Infirmary for Women and Children in order to complete her clinical requirements for a medical degree. She returned to Johns Hopkins at the end of this year to begin a three-year residency in psychiatry at the Phipps Clinic under Adolf Meyer. The period initiated a warm relationship with Harry Stack Sullivan, one of the major influences of her career in psychiatry. In her last year of residency at the clinic she became an instructor in psychiatry at the medical school. Subsequently, she began psychoanalytic treatment with Dr. Joseph C. Thompson—a development that ultimately brought about her estrangement from Meyer, her mentor, and caused her dismissal from Phipps Clinic.

She began private practice in Baltimore, and for two years taught mental hygiene at the Institute of Euthenics at Vassar College. The summers of 1928 and 1929 were spent studying abroad, in Budapest, with Sándor Ferenczi, whom she had met at the New School for Social Research in New York. In 1931 she returned to Budapest to remain for two years. Returning, she shifted her base from Baltimore to New York. Earlier, in 1930, she had been elected the first president of the pioneering Washington-Baltimore Psychoanalytic Society, organized by Harry Stack Sullivan.

Her activities in New York brought her again into close contact with Sullivan, and with a new friend, Karen Horney.

By 1938 she was very much involved in teaching at

the New York Institute and with the strong rivalries and tensions that had developed there between two opposing factions—those who adhered to the early rigid formulations of the libido theory and those who accepted the new thinking developed by Karen Horney and Erich Fromm. She was devoted to Fromm, who later psychoanalyzed her, and she greatly admired Karen Horney for her penetrating observations and pithy style. Throughout the controversy, she was on their side.

Early in 1941 the group of analysts at the New York Institute who opposed the new thinking had grown powerful enough to dismiss Karen Horney as a training analyst there. She had previously been censured by not being allowed to teach beginning students. Her entire training function was limited to a seminar for advanced students. Many of the faculty and students were outraged by this blatant violation of academic freedom. Karen Horney resigned, and Clara Thompson and three other faculty members resigned with her in protest against the Institute's action.

In 1943 the William Alanson White Psychiatric Foundation reorganized its Washington School of Psychiatry to include the group that had resigned from the New York Institute. By the fall of that year, under the leadership of Clara Thompson, Erich Fromm, Frieda Fromm-Reichmann, Harry Stack Sullivan, and Janet and David Rioch, a New York branch of the Washington School had been established with Clara Thompson as its executive director. The curriculum set up for the training of psychoanalysts here, as in the Washington school, integrated psychoanalysis with anthropology, political science, and social psychology. As in the Washington school also, a similarly integrated curriculum was provided for teachers, social workers, ministers, and others who needed the insight and understanding that this kind of training would give them in the performance of their professional functions.

The period that followed was a deeply satisfying one for Clara Thompson both in her personal and in her professional life.

Of her personal life during this period, it is sufficient to say that she had formed a deep and satisfying liaison—it was never formalized as a marriage—with the painter Henry Major, and her summers were spent with him at her vacation home in Provincetown from 1938 until his death in 1948.

The stormier episodes of a professional career marked by sharp divisions within the psychiatric camp are too well known to the profession and of too little import at this date to the general reading public to require repetition here. What stands out is her courage and unswerving loyalty to both friends and professional ideals. She continued her work with the Institute, her lectures, her private practice, and her writing—a highly influential flow of papers, articles, critiques, and reviews that includes the material in this volume—until her terminal illness in the summer of 1958. The diagnosis was cirrhosis of the liver, but it is not certain that it deceived her, for she had remarked some while earlier: "If it is what I think it is, there's nothing to do."

It was, as she had surmised, cancer.

She died on December 20, 1958.

Notes and References

Biologic Aspects

[1]Thompson's description of the varieties of orgasm has been borne out by the research of Masters and Johnson, who have exploded the myth of the so-called vaginal orgasm by demonstrating that all female orgasm involves clitoral stimulation of one kind or another. Anatomically, in coitus, the clitoris is stimulated by any stretching or contraction of the vaginal walls and labia.

The Role of Women in This Culture

[2]In 1831, after visiting America, Alexis de Tocqueville commented on the difference between American and European women:

Long before an American girl arrives at the marriageable age, her emancipation from maternal control begins: she has scarcely ceased to be a child, when she already thinks for herself, speaks with freedom, and acts on her own impulses. The great scene of the world is constantly open to her view: far from seeking to conceal it from her, it is every day disclosed more completely, and she is taught to survey it with a firm and calm gaze.

Thus the vices and dangers of society are early revealed to her; as she sees them clearly, she views them without illusion, and braves them without fear; for she is full of reliance on her own strength, and her confidence seems to be shared by all around her.

An American girl scarcely ever displays that virginal softness in the midst of young desires, or that innocent and ingenuous grace, which usually attend the European woman in the transition from girlhood to youth. It is rare that an American woman, at any age, displays childish timidity or ignorance. Like the young women of Europe, she seeks to please, but she knows precisely the cost of pleasing. If she does not abandon herself to evil, at least she knows that it exists; and she is remarkable rather for purity of manners than for chastity of mind. . . .

[U]nder these circumstances, believing that they had little chance of repressing in woman the most vehement passions of the human heart, they held that the surer way was to teach her the art of combatting those passions for herself. As they could not permit her virtue from being exposed to frequent danger, they determined that she should know how best to defend it; and more reliance was placed on the free vigor of her will than on safeguards which had been shaken or overthrown. Instead then of inculcating mistrust of herself, they constantly seek to enhance her confidence in her own strength of character. As it is neither possible nor desirable to keep a young woman in perpetual and complete ignorance, they hasten to give her a precocious knowledge in all subjects. Far from hiding the corruptions of the world from her, they prefer that she should see them at once, and train herself to shun them; and they hold it of more importance to protect her conduct, than to be overscrupulous of the innocence of her thoughts. . . .

I am aware that an education of this kind is not

without danger; I am sensible that it tends to invigorate the judgment at the expense of the imagination, and to make cold and virtuous women instead of affectionate wives and agreeable companions to man. Society may be more tranquil and better regulated, but domestic life has often fewer charms. These, however, are secondary evils, which may be braved for the sake of higher interests. At the stage at which we are now arrived, the choice is no longer left to us; a democratic education is indispensable to protect women from the dangers with which democratic institutions and manners surround them.

In America, the independence of woman is irrecoverably lost in the bonds of matrimony. If an unmarried woman is less constrained there than elsewhere, a wife is subjected to stricter obligations. The former makes her father's house an abode of freedom and of pleasure; the latter lives in the home of her husband as if it were a cloister. Yet these two different conditions of life are perhaps not so contrary as may be supposed, and it is natural that the American woman should pass through the one to arrive at the other.

Religious communities and trading nations entertain peculiarly curious notions of marriage: the former consider the regularity of woman's life as the best pledge and most certain sign of the purity of her morals; the latter regard it as the highest security for the order and prosperity of the household. The Americans are, at the same time, a puritanical people and a commercial nation; their religious opinions, as well as their trading habits, consequently lead them to require much abnegation on the part of women, and a constant sacrifice of her pleasures to her duties which is seldom demanded of her in Europe. Thus, in the United States, the inexorable opinion of the public carefully circumscribes woman within the narrow circle of domestic interests and duties, and forbids her to step beyond it. (*Democracy in America,*

Richard Heffner, ed. [Alexis de Tocqueville, New York: New American Library, 1956], p. 234.)

[3]Here, Clara Thompson is drawing on her own unhappy experience as well as observation. Before she had completed college, she met a major in the United States Army Medical Corps, who fell in love with her, and proposed marriage. As it developed, however, the young major's proposal was conditional: He required that she give up her medical career. She refused, and on that issue they broke off. She was deeply troubled by the decision during her years in medical school, feeling guilty toward the man she had rejected, and uncertain of her future as a woman doctor. It was not until 1938, when she was forty-five years old, that she had the good fortune to meet a man with whom she could enter into a fulfilling and enduring relationship.

[4]A contemporary historian, Henry Steele Commager, spoke for the consensus in 1950 when he wrote:

Twentieth century America, even more than Nineteenth, seemed to be a woman's country. The supremacy of woman could be read in the statistics of property ownership, insurance, education, or literature, or in the advertisements of any popular magazine. Women ran the schools and the churches, they determined what would appear in the magazines and the movies and what would be heard over the radio. As many girls as boys attended college, and women made their way successfully into almost every profession. There were a hundred magazines designed especially for their entertainment or edification, and among them some with the largest circulation, while most metropolitan newspapers had a page for women and every radio station a series of programs directed exclusively to their supposed needs. As women spent most of the money, the overwhelming body of advertisements was addressed to them, and advertisers found it advisable to introduce the feminine motive even, or especially where they hoped to attract men. Traditionally women had ruled the home, but only in America did they design it, build it, furnish it, direct its activities, and fix its standards. Most American children knew more of their mothers' than of their fathers' families, and it was the opinion of many observers of World War II that the silver cord bound American youth more firmly than the youth of any other land. (Henry Steele Commager, *The American Mind* [New Haven: Yale University Press, 1950], p. 424.)

Cultural Pressures in the Psychology of Women

[5]Germaine Greer, in her recent book, *The Female Eunuch,* eloquently describes the vicissitudes of this struggle for independence as a woman without surrender to imitation of masculinity.

Some Effects of the Derogatory Attitude toward Female Sexuality

[6]McClelland has recently documented the powerful pernicious effects of such attitudes in his chapter, "Wanted: A New Self-Image for Women," in *The Woman in America*; R. J. Lifton, ed., Houghton Mifflin, New York, 1965; 173–192.

Selected Bibliography

1941
"The Role of Women in This Culture," *Psychiatry*, IV,
    1–8.
Bibliography: Clara Thompson, *Psychiatry*, IV, 145.

1942
"Cultural Pressures in the Psychology of Women," *Psychiatry*, V; 331–339.
"The Relation of the Medical Man to the Neurotic
    Patient," *Medical Record*, CLV, 277–280.

1943
"Penis Envy in Woman," *Psychiatry*, VI, 123–125.
Review: *Leadership and Isolation*, by Helen Hall Jennings. *Psychiatry*, VI, 448.

1944
Review: *The Psychology of Women: A Psychoanalytical Interpretation*, Vol. I, by Helene Deutsch.
    Newsletter, American Association Psychiatric Social Workers, XIV, 56–57.

1947
Review: *The Psychology of Women: A Psychoanalytical Interpretation*, Vol. II, by Helene Deutsch.
    Journal of Psychiatric Social Work, XVI, 101.

"Changing Concepts of Homosexuality in Psychoanalysis," *Psychiatry*, X, 183–189.

Bibliography: Clara Thompson, *Psychiatry*, X, 237–238.

1948

Review: *About the Kinsey Report*, Donald Porter Geddes and Enid Curie, eds. *Psychiatry*, XI, 407.

1949

"Cultural Conflicts of Women in Our Society," *Samiksa*, III, 125–134.

"Harry Stack Sullivan, the Man," *Psychiatry*, XII, 435–437.

1950

Psychoanalysis: Evolution and Development (with Patrick Mullahy) (New York: Hermitage House, 1950).

"Some Effects of the Derogatory Attitude toward Female Sexuality," *Psychiatry*, XIII, 349–354.

"Cultural Complications in the Sexual Life of Women," *Symposium on Feminine Psychology, March 18–19, 1950*, p. 54. Department of Psychiatry, Psychoanalytic Division, New York Medical College—Flower and Fifth Avenue Hospitals.

"Sex and Adolescence," *Consumer Reports*, XV, 365–366.

1959

"The Unmarried Woman," *Pastoral Psychology*, X, 44–45.

1961

"Femininity," in Albert Ellis and Albert Abarbanel, eds., *The Encyclopedia of Sexual Behavior* (New York: Hawthorn Books, 1961).

Index

187

sexual frankness, 47
sexual freedom, 121, 122
sexual frustration, 22
sexual ignorance, 120
sexual intimacy, 46
sexual life, importance of, 148, 149
sexual organs, functioning of, 45
sexual response, 19, 20
sexual restriction, 102
sexual revolution, 46
sexual revulsion, 69, 70
sexual satisfaction, 121
sexual tension, 22, 23, 24, 85
sexuality, derogation of, 150
"sissy" traits, 80, 88, 104, 105
small families, 119
social dependency, 141
social institutions, 116
social isolation, 123
social life, restrictions of, 116
social restrictions, 130
social taboo, 61, 62, 83, 101, 103, 110
somatic difficulties, 162
sphincter, 151
sphincter, anal, 45
sphincter control, 150, 151
sphincter morality, 150
status, change of, 116
stimulation, anal, 89
strange creatures, 104
Studies in Hysteria, 111
sublimated satisfaction, 118
sublimation, 99, 100
submission, 138
submissiveness, 139

subordination of woman's interests, 141
suffragettes, 91
Sullivan, Harry Stack, 27, 44, 45, 176, 177
superego, 126, 133, 134
superego, stern, 102
superego, weak, 100, 102, 103

Tauber, Edward S., 22
Thompson, Clara Mabel, 73, 175, 176, 177, 178
Thompson, Dr. Joseph C., 176
thymus gland, 164
thyroid gland, 165
Titian, 164
toilet training, 33
tomboy, 80, 88, 104, 105
traumata, 140
traumatic experiences, 61, 64, 77

underprivilege, 141
urination, 35
urine, 150
uterus, malpositions of, 25, 52

vagina, 21, 22, 34, 37, 38, 89, 126, 127, 133
vaginal muscles, 151
vaginismus, 147
virgin, 23
virginity, 121

white hair, 164
White, William Alanson, 176
"wolf," 87
World War I, 46, 114